Rise of Dragons – Book 3

Equinox Betrayal

G Clatworthy

Find more at www.gemmaclatworthy.com

Cover art by Sanjay Charlon (Beehive Illustrations)

Foreword

Thank you to the amazing first readers, terrific typo hunters and grammar gurus – you are awesome!

This series is for my D&D group whose stories always inspire me!

Please join me on patreon at www.patreon.com/G_Clatworthy, or on Instagram at www.instagram.com/gemmaclatworthy or join the conversation at Gemma's book wyrms facebook group.

Chapter 1

I leapt to the left to avoid the dagger aiming straight for my face. Crouching low, I kicked out at the elf's knee. She spun away easily and came at me again. I parried with Bane, my double headed axe, then adjusted my grip and swung back. She was expecting it and somersaulted out of the way. Bloody elven agility. She danced around me, tossing her dagger from hand to hand.

"Try and hit me!" she taunted. I hung back, catching my breath and weighing up my options. She was faster than me and more agile and better with her weapon. I, on the other hand, was smaller than her. Not much of an advantage there.

I rushed in, she sidestepped in time for me to overbalance and stumble. In an instant she was on me. She twisted my arm painfully, forcing me to drop my axe and then pushed me to the ground. I was expecting it and went down fast, using my weight to pull her with me. I clocked the surprise in her eyes as she staggered forward. I pulled my own dagger from my belt with my free arm and brought it round. She dived into a forward roll, still holding my arm. I cried out as my arm was wrenched forward of her volition and I did my own clumsy version of a somersault. Red stars clouded my vision from the pain of the arm bar.

She kicked out at my other hand, her long leg easily allowing her to reach my wrist. I felt the blade drop from my hand. I blinked as I felt cold steel against my neck. It was over.

She held the knife there for a second then released me.

"Not bad, you're getting faster," a rare compliment, "but if you're going to try surprise, make sure your opponent doesn't still have you in an arm bar."

I grunted in between panting as I tried to get my breath back. Espretha was unflustered and annoyingly looked even more attractive with a slight flush to her face from the training session. I pushed myself up and adjusted my sports bra. It was a small feat of engineering to support my curvy bust, and it was always digging in uncomfortably somewhere. At least it stopped the embarrassing jiggling that had caused more than a few jaws to drop when the elf had forced me to jog round the park as a warm up for our first session.

I walked over to where Errol, my pet wyrm, was sunbathing on our bags near a tree. He grumbled softly as I dislodged him to get to my water bottle. I wiped the sweat out of my eyes and took a swig. Then I dug around in my backpack for a chocolate bar. I started to tear into the wrapper and just got it open when Espretha knocked it from my hand.

"Hey!"

"While I'm teaching you, I'm in charge of your body and you are not putting that stuff in your mouth!"

I picked up the chocolate, brushing off a blade of grass and wondering how bad it would be if I ate it after it had been on the floor, "Training's over, and you might be in charge of my body but you are not in charge of what I eat," I protested.

The elf tapped her foot thoughtfully, "Training's over when I say it's over…I think we'll finish with a jog." I groaned loudly. Espretha's idea of a light jog was a run around the park. My shorter legs always struggled to keep up with her and I was already exhausted. Note to self: do not provoke sadistic elf. She smiled nastily and picked up her backpack.

"I should take Errol back…" I tried.

She gave the plump wyrm a look of disgust, "He needs to lose weight too, he can come with us."

She set off. I groaned again, but I was learning a lot in these training sessions and secretly it was nice to be bullied into taking exercise. I was still curvy, but I was more toned than I had been a couple of months ago when we had started these lessons.

I clipped on Errol's chain link lead, "Sorry boy, looks like we're going for another run."

He looked up at me reproachfully but got up and trotted alongside me, jumping every so often so he could glide in the warm air. Lucky wyrm with his wings. Espretha stayed just ahead of me as we followed a circuit around Bute Park.

I would have made snarky comments behind her back but I was far too out of breath to do anything but struggle on.

After the run, Espretha made sure we stretched out our muscles, then it was time for my favourite part. I was aching all over but I perked up as we left the leafy park straight into Cardiff city centre. I ignored the creepy stone animal statues that lined the walls of Bute Park and the construction noises coming from inside Cardiff Castle where they were rebuilding the destruction caused by a waking a slumbering dragon earlier in the year. I was laser focused on our destination: the Dragon's Head café. Home of heavenly syrupy coffee and the best brownies in the city.

I entered first and collapsed onto the counter. Brinda, the owner, smiled at me, "Coffee?"

"With extra syrup," I panted, "and two of your brownies."

"Tea for me," Espretha had barely broken a sweat. Sometimes I really hated her. She took a seat at one of the mismatched tables and lounged. Elves always made themselves immediately at home wherever they were.

I sank into the opposite seat and waited, studiously not looking at the pictures of famous people hung on the walls. Brinda had conspired with my mother to get my picture on there after I'd been featured in the Cardiff paper when the first dragon had awakened and now there was a picture of me looking dishevelled, to put it mildly, hanging brightly on the wall. I had refused to autograph it.

Brinda bustled over quickly with our order and a small bowl of water and a biscuit shaped like a dragon for Errol. He licked her hand then starting lapping the water noisily under the table.

"That was a good session," Espretha commented as she sipped her tea delicately. I inhaled deeply, savouring the bittersweet aroma of my coffee and grunted my assent.

"How's business?" she asked, carefully not meeting my eyes. This was how it always started.

"It's OK. Aloora's had to teach me more about managing a social media account now everyone wants a picture in my shop. The hashtags are a nightmare."

She winced at the mention of my gnomish friend. Good. She should feel guilty that she kidnapped Aloora earlier this year. I wasn't sure I could ever forgive her for that, but Aloora had been surprisingly sanguine about Espretha contacting me and I trusted my friend even if I didn't entirely trust the elf.

She nibbled at the brownie I pushed in front of her. She never ordered her own, but I was determined to convert her to unhealthy ways and, as my Mum always said, "Fatten up your friends and it will make you look slimmer!" I'd always laughed about that but in hindsight I had been a chubby teenager.

"You're getting a lot of business from that…painting…though?" she visibly stopped herself from shuddering.

I hated the huge mural that my so-called friend Marco had painted on my shop wall. He'd created a buxom dwarf that sort of looked like me, with a beard! It was monstrous but he was my friend and I leapt to its defence, "Yeah. It's trending all over Cardiff! I'm lucky I've got such good friends."

Another wince. It was petty but after training sessions, I always liked to provoke her. It was my way of getting my own back.

"A lot of supernatural beings like the picture?"

This was what I had been waiting for. She always tried to be subtle but really she wanted information about Lorandir. An elven customer turned friend of mine who had helped me rescue Aloora and had tried to stop the cult that Espretha had joined. We hadn't been successful at stopping them awakening a dragon, and her childhood friend had cut her out of his life.

"Yep," I took a long drink of my syrupy coffee, savouring the sweet flavour. I couldn't resist trying to provoke her, "Lorandir was in the shop the other day…"

"I saw…in one of your posts." I nodded brightly. She was stalking him on social media then. Good to know. "Does he know about our training sessions?" she asked, a little too nonchalantly.

Schiztz. I had been enjoying tormenting her but hadn't actually got around to telling him I was hanging out with his ex-friend, who had kidnapped my friend and who we had fought together. I mean, how do you break that news without sounding completely crazy? And I was enjoying getting to know Lorandir.

I pulled out my phone to check the time and did a double take. Saved by the time! "I have to go! I promised Aloora I'd help her with apartment hunting. Sorry Espretha, got to go!"

I downed my coffee and took the remains of my brownie to go. Errol protested as I tugged him out of the door, shouted goodbye to Brinda and hobbled back to my shop cum flat. I left Errol tucking into a small bucket of coal and had a quick shower before texting Aloora and walking to the taxi rank. I was too late to be able to catch a bus so would have to get one of the licensed cars to take me instead. A lot of people were on the streets today and there seemed to be a lot of red and blue shirts around. The colours of the Welsh rugby team and the Cardiff blues football team. I guessed there was a match somewhere. Not at the stadium of course – that was being used as a nesting ground by the dragons. An American couple nudged my shoulder as they passed. The man in a plaid red shirt with stubble that might be called a beard in the right light spoke by my ear.

"Gee, it's just like the movies ain't it?"

The wife nodded blankly as her husband took a photo of a large magical ward etched onto a building; part of the city's efforts to reassure its citizens that they were safe. From the look on her face, I guessed it was about the thousandth time he'd stopped to capture the city with his camera.

Aloora replied with the address, distracting me from the couple. It was the third time she'd sent it to me. Then a string of emojis, including a clock and a surprised face. I got the message and quickened my pace, my tired muscles protesting.

Chapter 2

Aloora was standing outside a sleek apartment building, tapping her foot and scrolling on her smartphone, frowning slightly.

"Sorry, sorry!" I held up my hands.

She waved her own hand dismissively and typed something into her phone before putting it into her leather satchel, embossed with a dragon design. "Who does he think he is?"

"Who?" I was not following this at all.

"This guy 'Denalth72' has the nerve to tell me that the dragon we saw fly out of the ground at Stonehenge, which is still being repaired, was a collective hallucination!" She was talking about one of her social media accounts then, it was starting to make more sense. Aloora, known online as Aloora Dragonquest, was a minor celebrity in Cardiff thanks to her social media accounts that focused on her academic research into dragons. Of course, now that dragons were back in the world, her following had rocketed and instead of like-minded folk, she was also dealing with everyday conspiracy theorists.

"What did you tell him?"

"I told him that I thought it was odd he was believing the government cover stories of gas explosions and bomb scares, after all that's what they want you to think!"

I laughed, "Brilliant! You'll have him rethinking his entire life with that!"

She grinned wickedly, then gestured to the building, "The agent's already upstairs with Marco. Come on."

She trotted upstairs impatiently, not even thinking about taking the lift. I forced myself to follow her as my legs protested at the stairs. She kept going. How many floors did this building have? I gripped the handrail and forced myself to continue. I was panting by the time she finally left the stairwell and opened a heavy fire safety door. She made impatient signals with her hands and tapped her foot as she waited for me to catch up. I wheezed as I passed her.

"Hard training session today?"

I nodded. I couldn't speak.

"Still enjoying working with Espretha then?"

"Enjoy is a strong word…" I gasped.

"I was thinking…maybe I should meet her…you know, not as a victim."

I didn't know what to say to that. A flurry of expressions crossed my face. I was never good at hiding my feelings.

She sighed, “I know, it’s probably a bad idea, but her case file made it seem like this cult thing really was a blip and I’d like to ask her why she did it.”

“You know more about her than I do,” I settled for a non-committal, neutral response.

She nodded thoughtfully, then knocked sharply on a smart, white door, “Here’s the apartment.”

A keen estate agent opened the door instantly and ushered us in. I blinked as I took in the place. Light streamed in from the large windows, framing perfect views of the water in Cardiff Bay. Aloora gave it an appraising glance then started opening cupboards and doors.

I wondered, not for the first time, just how much her new job at the Magical Liaison Office was paying. Enough for her to leave the shabby student house share she was currently living in for sure, but enough for a swanky flat like this, wow!

I thought about the strange stain on the ceiling of my own bedroom and the growing patch of mould in the bathroom. This place was a palace. The open plan living room and kitchen was clean and modern. I pulled myself away from the fantastic views and walked into a bedroom.

A king-sized bed filled the space, illuminated by another large picture window. I opened a mirrored door and found a neat wardrobe filled with somebody’s suits. Another door led to a huge en-suite, including a bathtub. I was jealous. I hadn’t had a bath since I’d moved into my place. My small shower with temperamental water pressure suddenly seemed totally inadequate.

Marco walked in and plonked himself on the bed, “It is fabulous, no?” his Italian accent curled around the words.

I nodded and sank down next to him, “Perfectly perfect.”

“I think I will have this room,” he looked around and then lay fully on the bed.

I laughed at him already making himself at home here and went to find my best friend. She was standing on the small balcony, leaning on the metallic railing and looking across the water dreamily.

I joined her, trying not to think about the height. I had never been a fan of them, and put it down to my dwarven heritage. “Marco’s already moving in!”

“He’s not having the room with the views!” she replied indignantly, “Not when I’m paying the most rent!”

I put my hands up in mock surrender, “Hey, don’t shoot the messenger!”

I smiled. It was kind of her to help Marco leave the student house too, but as he was such a good cook, I was sure there was a slight ulterior motive. I admit it, I was jealous that my two friends were going to live in this gorgeous apartment, far enough away that I couldn’t walk over and see them. Maybe I should get a bike.

“What do you think? Be honest,” she broke into my thoughts.

I pretended to consider carefully, “Well it’s almost as good as the place with the seventies wallpaper, but you don’t have as nice views as the one that overlooked the train tracks…”

She laughed, "There's another room you know, if you wanted to move here too," her voice softened and she searched my face, breaking into my thoughts, "I mean, I was going to turn it into a library slash study, but I'd love it if you lived here too...and honestly, we could do with a third person in on the rent. Even with prices down thanks to the dragons nesting in the Millennium Stadium, it's still expensive."

It was a lie, but a nice one to save my pride and make me think I was doing her a favour, rather than the other way around. "I'll think about it," I promised.

She nodded, satisfied with that. It was tempting and certainly a lot nicer than my flat. But my unofficial living arrangements above my shop in Royal Arcade were so convenient and then there was the rent. I was getting my shop for a bargain price after I helped out the Arcade's owner with a kobold problem. The estate agent tried to hand Aloora a card as we left the building. He looked pretty desperate to get the place rented out and I guessed the exodus of people leaving a dragon-infested city was taking its toll on estate agents. I had insisted on taking the lift and was stealthily massaging my sore thighs as I tried to soothe my muscles while I waited for them to finish up. She brushed him away saying she did everything online. That was true.

"We'll let you know, we have other viewings," she said coolly and started to walk away. I followed her, trying not to wince as my legs protested. Marco took the card and gave him a small wink then walked behind the building to the carpark. He was the only man I knew who walked like a model, and dressed like one too. We piled into Marco's small, ancient Volkswagen and he set off. BBC Radio 4 blared out of the speakers. He insisted it helped him to learn English, but more likely the radio was stuck on that channel.

"We are taking the apartment," Marco stated it as a fact.

"Of course we are!"

"Don't act too keen, you might be able to get the rent down, especially as no one else wants to live in Cardiff right now," I chimed in, my business head chiming in. Or maybe it was my dwarven ancestry, or maybe I was just cheap.

"Then we must 'ave dinner to celebrate!"

Aloora looked at the clock on his car, "Bit early for food isn't it?"

It was never too early for me to eat, I was firmly on Marco's side and he drove the short distance to a carpark nearer the eateries in the Mermaid Quay part of the bay. Chic, sleek buildings housed new restaurants after this part of the bay had been redeveloped. The glass fronts reflected the low sun and dazzled passers-by. As we approached the restaurants, I gave the metallic mermaid statue that presided over the water a rub for good luck as we passed, admiring the sculpture's metal work. There were some seriously nice restaurants and all were, surprisingly, open in the mid-afternoon. We settled on a brasserie with seating outside and ordered cocktails, or a mocktail in Marco's case, and appetisers while we watched the water. It shone a sapphire blue in the late afternoon sun and I enjoyed the slight cooling breeze coming in from the sea. There weren't many other people around. I guessed trade picked up later in the evening, unless the dragons had put people off coming to the bay. A helicopter flew past, strangely low as we ate. The whirring noise of its propellers cut across our conversation. Aloora frowned at it as it passed overhead and checked her phone. We left soon after that and Marco drove us back towards the city. There was a roadblock in place as we got closer to the centre and he swore in Italian. Aloora asked him to wait while she got out to talk to the uniformed officer about the roadblock. She flashed her ID confirming she was a member of the Magical Liaison Office and he started talking.

She leaned in through the window of the small car, "Something's going on with the dragons. I'm going to walk from here, there's something happening at the stadium."

I got out of the car too, "I'm going that way anyway, I'll walk with you." My legs weren't happy about that decision, but I had to get home somehow.

Aloora nodded, "Sure. Marco, go home, you'll have to go the long way round, these roadblocks are all over the city centre. I'll grab a lift back with one of the Liaison team later."

We hurried past the roadblock. The officer gave me a look but didn't stop us. My heart started to beat faster as we got closer to the Millennium Stadium, where the dragons had made their home after being awakened earlier in the year.

There were now three of them: two adults and one smaller dragon. They frequently circled the city and had destroyed a number of buses and the Student Union steps over the few months they had lived here. It was a miracle that there had been no serious casualties, but the dragons didn't seem to want to eat people, preferring to fish over the sea or steal cattle from local farmers. It was clear that humans and dragons were not compatible, but no one was going to tell a huge creature that could breathe fire or ice it had to leave. Not even the football and rugby fans who frequently lamented the loss of their beloved grounds to the dragons. I could hear their chanting now. So it was the people who were starting to leave, pushing down the prices of flats like the one we'd seen earlier in the afternoon. I shook my head. Nope I could still hear chanting. What the dzrak was going on?

Thousands of sports fans in blue and red thronged through the streets. I gaped. I had never seen the city this busy, not even on a match day. I stared at one of the cardboard signs a large rugby fan held aloft: it had a crude drawing of a dragon with a red cross over it. A protest. I hurried to catch up as my friend weaved her way through the crowd towards the dragons' nest. This could turn ugly fast. Our small sizes and well-placed used of elbows meant we got near the front quickly. I noted one of the posters the city council had put up promising the use of wizards to contain the dragons: *Protect the People* printed over a stylised picture of a powerful wizard. Wizards couldn't contain dragons but it was good propaganda to stop the exodus from the city. Someone had scrawled 'knob' over the wizard's hat. Not everyone was happy with magical folk living openly. I pushed on.

The air got colder as we approached the stadium. I shivered reflexively. My dwarven blood meant that I ran hotter than humans, but my breath began to appear in frosty white clouds thanks to the white ice dragon's impact on the local temperature. I shivered again, remembering my first experience of the dragon's frost when I was encased in ice at the Summer Solstice festival at Stonehenge. Not something I wanted to repeat.

"What are they doing?" Aloora pulled me out of my memories with her muttering. I glanced around and noticed several tanks parked around the stadium, their guns pointing towards the arena. Soldiers were keeping the protestors back with limited success.

My friend pulled out her phone and made a call. I heard the sharp tones of Special Agent Jones as she picked up.

"What's going on?" she barked, loud enough that I could hear.

"Are you here?" Aloora replied, scanning the area for her boss.

"You know I'm not. I'm still on leave."

"Who's authorised this then?"

"Who's authorised what?" I could imagine Agent Jones pinching the bridge of her nose in annoyance. She was not easily patient.

"There are tanks outside the dragon's nest." Hearing Aloora say it out loud sounded absurd and I looked around again. Yep, absurd, but accurate.

A stream of Dwarfish curse words sounded from the phone. I was impressed, usually only people who had grown up speaking the language could cuss so fluently.

“Try to stop them doing anything stupid. I’ll make some calls.” Agent Jones hung up abruptly.

“Let’s find whoever’s in charge here.” My friend squared her shoulders and set off towards a group of soldiers standing behind the tanks. One of them held a pair of binoculars and was staring intently at the stadium.

Chapter 3

A clean shaven man in a military uniform was barking orders at people as we approached. He didn't notice us at first, but we both had pointy elbows and, being under the eye line of the average person, we managed to get close enough to talk to him.

"What's going on here?" Aloora demanded. I stood slightly behind her as back up. Although I wasn't sure what exactly I was going to do to help. I wished I was holding my ancestral axe, but I'd left it behind, thinking that we could handle estate agents without weaponry.

The man looked us both up and down, taking in my heavy duty leather, gothic-style boots, faded jeans and green leather jacket. Aloora was looking even less intimidating in leggings, pixie boots and a fitted t-shirt dress that had a dragon embroidered on it. The dragon was reading a book.

"How did you get here? This is a restricted area," he waved at two of his cronies, "take them away."

He started to turn but Aloora was already thrusting her Magical Liaison Office identification in his face. "I'm with the MLO. We have jurisdiction over all things magical, including dragons. Why are you aiming guns at their nest? We're in the process of having that made into a protected site."

He sighed heavily, "Well, Ms…" he squinted at the ID, "...Dragonquest, is that your real name?"

Aloora shrugged. She was doing a good job of acting cool, considering as far as I knew, her job at the Office was mostly researching dragons, which fit nicely with her ongoing PhD studies.

"OK Ms Dragonquest, we're under orders from the government to clear the dragons out of the city. They're too dangerous and the government has jurisdiction over both of our branches."

"What are you going to do?" I asked incredulously, "Blast them out?"

He shrugged this time, "It's classified...and you are?"

I kept my mouth shut, wavering under his cold gaze and Aloora answered with her own question, "Who do I need to call to put a stop to this nonsense?"

The man blinked, unused to being spoken to like this by anyone, let alone a petite gnome with ink stains on her fingers. "I take my orders from the Ministry of Defence." He turned his back on us then and lifted a pair of binoculars to his eyes.

I squinted into the twilight, my eyes were pretty good in the dark, thanks to my dwarven heritage but I couldn't see anything useful. I could hear a lot of shouting though and the atmosphere was tense. I didn't know whether the crowd supported the military but they were angry. Aloora had retreated back to the safety of a doorway where we could lurk unnoticed by the military personnel. I followed her hastily, not wanting to be asked tough questions like who I was and what I was doing here. I heard the twang of an American accent carry across the street.

"Well gee, look at that honey! Regular British tanks. Hey, d'ya reckon I could get a photo up close?"

"JR, come on, we have to get back to the hotel to make our dinner reservations?"

I thought I saw a plaid shirt shining under the streetlights. I shook my head at tourists getting stuck in the middle of a riot. Hopefully JR would listen to his wife and head back to the hotel before any trouble started. The shouts from the protestors were already getting louder and more irate. The tension was building like electricity. I rubbed my arms. This was going badly. I heard a scraping sound and more shouting. Soldiers were lining up at one of the blockades. More shouting and then a police van pulled up. Officers with riot gear poured out and ran over to the noise. I shrank back into our doorway, wanting to stay unnoticed.

The screen from Aloora's phone illuminated her face as she googled the Ministry of Defence for a contact number. She dialled a number, then was put on hold. Sighing in frustration, she switched apps and started tweeting to her many followers about dragon rights in Cardiff. Her social media feeds lit up.

I watched as the man in charge got his own phone call. He turned and his eyes swept across the buildings where we were standing. He hung up and marched over. Schiztz.

"What do you think you're doing putting this on social media?" His voice was loud and it took a lot not to lean back from the sheer force of being shouted at by a large man in uniform.

Aloora shrugged, "I answer to the Magical Liaison Office."

He glowered at her, then shouted to two men, "Take them out of here!"

"Hey!" My friend started to protest, but we were unceremoniously grabbed by thc arms. They began to frogmarch us away from the stadium when the noise started. It was a low rumble that ramped up into an ear splitting shriek. The shouts from the crowd quieted as they took it in.

The soldiers paused and looked back at the dragons' nest. "Uh-oh," whispered Aloora. The scream came again, followed by a more human shout of terror. The protestors picked up the panic and their shouts turned to cries of help as they fought to get away. Aloora shook off the soldier and ran back to the general in charge. "What did you do?" she shouted at him.

His face had paled at the sound of the dragons' ire. Taken aback at being shouted at by such a small person, he answered, "I sent a recon team in."

"Idiot!" she replied.

I took the opportunity to wrench my own arm free and joined them, "What's going on Ally?"

"Dragon's are territorial and possessive and they've made their home in that building. Those soldiers have just lost their lives because you didn't think and you didn't ask anyone, you just followed military protocol, which is absolutely insufficient for dealing with dragons!" she prodded him on his bulletproof vest.

"You don't know they're dead," he blustered.

Aloora nodded, "Oh yes I do. I barely survived a dragon attack earlier this year and she's survived two, and we had magical weapons. Let me guess, you sent them in with some sort of standard issue gun?"

He nodded dumbly.

"Er, guys," I broke into Aloora's tirade. She glared at me before following my gaze and looking upwards. The dragons had taken to the sky. They swooped in lazy circles overhead, taking in the tanks and soldiers surrounding them. I heard screams as the crowd saw the dragons too. The tension slipped into pure panic. Someone shot a firework into the sky. It exploded, showering sparks around the flying reptiles. I heard more screams as people tried to flee, starting a stampede back away from the stadium.

The general pushed his hat back, exposing his neat, grey haircut and started talking into a radio. The tanks raised their gun barrels so they were pointing at the sky. The red dragon dived suddenly and spewed fire directly onto the tanks. The armoured vehicles survived, but I imagined it was pretty toasty inside for the crews. Two jeeps nearby didn't fare as well as their tyres melted in the heat of the blast.

People raced for the cover provided by the nearest buildings. In the chaos, the dragon swooped again. I heard a burst of gunfire from somewhere close by and the dragon gave a mighty roar before turning and sending another wave of flames in the direction of the shooter. I winced and hoped the soldier had found some cover.

"JR! This is not TV! You get your ass back over here and away from those creatures now!"

"Gee honey, don't be a spoilsport. These tanks remind me of my second tour in Afghanistan. Just let me get one close up picture then we'll go."

I stared as the American in the plaid shirt strode closer to the burning vehiclcs, angling his large, almost obnoxiously sized camera at the tanks. I had no idea how he got past the barricades. The larger white dragon now joined the fracas and swooped low, picking up one of the tanks and dropping it on another with a resounding crash. It did a circuit of the Millennium Stadium. JR stopped focusing on the armoured vehicles and followed the dragon with his camera. I shouted a warning and took a step towards him. Too late. On its return, it shot out a blast of icy breath at the tower of tanks, encasing them and JR with thick ice crystals. I stopped and retreated back to the shelter of the wall. Perhaps he'd survive if they could thaw him out.

I was debating trying to defrost him with the fire enchantment bespelled onto my axe when a soldier nearby hefted a rocket launcher onto his shoulder and aimed at the white dragon. I heard a whoosh then an explosion as it hit the creature directly on the stomach. The dragon whirled backwards at the force of the impact then flapped its huge wings, soaring upwards into the darkening sky.

I pushed Aloora and we scrambled to get further away from the soldier as the dragon dived. He turned and ran, but there was nowhere he could go. This time, instead of the icy blast I was expecting, the dragon breathed a dark liquid at the soldier. He started screaming as it connected and burnt through his body armour.

"Poison sacs!" I heard Aloora exclaim, "That's the female!" She sounded excited at the discovery and I saw her take her phone out.

"Don't start filming!" I hissed. She ignored me and I could only hope she wasn't live streaming this.

A tall figure blurred into focus. I breathed a sigh of relief as Dot gave us a large grin, showing her vampire fangs. "What's occurring?" she asked as she took in the chaotic scene. Wrapped up in a chunky knit jumper and jeans, accessorised with one of the enchanted swords I had created for the Office's Summer Solstice mission, she was surprisingly calm for someone who had just legged it across the city.

"Dragons are fighting the army!" I blustered, stating the obvious.

"To be fair, the army started it," Aloora was firmly on the dragons' side.

Dot nodded, "Agent Jones called me. Do you think the dragons will stop the attack if the army backs off?"

I blinked but the question was clearly aimed at my friend, the dragon expert. Aloora shook her head, "No. They're territorial. If anything this will make them escalate their attacks on the city as they assert dominance in this area."

"That's what we worried about," she sighed, "in that case, we'll have to lure the dragons away."

“How exactly are we going to do that without getting ourselves killed?” my voice had gone up a couple of octaves as I contemplated entering the fray.

“Have you still got the recordings you made?” Dot ignored me and addressed Aloora, who nodded her head and shook her phone. Her entire life was on that thing.

“Send them to Agent Jones.” Aloora began frantically searching her phone and attaching sound files to emails, her large costume rings sparkling as they caught the light of the fires from the battle raging on the road.

I was slow on the uptake, “What’s the plan?”

Aloora’s fingers didn’t slow down as she replied, “It’s brilliant. The dragons will respond to other dragons. If we can play the right recordings, far enough away, they’ll leave the fight to seek out more of their own kind. That’s why the white dragons left Stonehenge instead of staying to fight us.”

I nodded along. I’d wondered why they hadn’t finished us off at the Solstice, choosing to fly away. Then a thought struck me, “How did you get the recordings?”

Aloora turned her hazel eyes to me and shrugged, still tapping at her phone, “I’ve been coming here and recording them. It’s a beautiful sound really, and I think I’ve caught some words in Draconic,” her eyes turned misty as she warmed to her favourite subject, “it’s amazing to hear the language being spoken by the original species. I was way off about some of the pronunciations and Professor Elrond’s been helping me translate, his hearing is a lot more sensitive than mine. Draconic is quite a tonal language.”

I groaned, the elven professor was the foremost living expert on dragons in the UK and it didn't surprise me that he and Aloora had been obsessed with the dragons. Aloora shrugged again, "What? He's been coming with me," she paused, her hand finally slowed on her phone's keyboard, "All sent. I've suggested she start with the first one, I think that's the mating call."

"Where are they going to go?" I needed details.

Dot smiled, "Agent Jones has made a few calls. My guess is the elves will help, or if not the highlands of Scotland might be free." I started laughing at the weak joke. I think I was slightly hysterical at the absurdity of the plan and experiencing my third dragon attack of the year.

I turned back to the fight, wishing I had Bane in my hands. I didn't actually want to join in with the battle, but the comfort of a weapon would have been nice. I would have felt less helpless.

"So what now?"

"Now we wait," Dot caught my look and gave another shrug, "that's all we can do."

I shifted restlessly, watching soldiers emerge from the shadows to take pot shots at creatures that didn't seem bothered by rockets, grenades or tank shells. Most of the civilian crowd had dispersed, although a few drunks were throwing beer bottles into the sky in the general direction of the dragons. I chuckled to myself when a bottle hit the lout who had thrown it on the way down. He swore loudly and wobbled his way away, back towards the city centre and probably another pub. Briefly I wondered why they hadn't thought to enchant their ammunition, but if the Magical

Liaison Office weren't involved in the plan, I guessed that wouldn't have occurred to them. And, I thought smugly, it wasn't as if just anyone could enchant metal, it took training and some natural magic attuned to metalwork. I flexed my fingers instinctively, wondering if I should offer my skills and help out.

Before I could step forward, I saw the red dragon flying low over the road, towards a soldier, who was outlined by a blaze from one of the jeeps. He was limping quickly and wasn't that far from us. Before I could process the thought, my legs were moving. I barrelled into the shocked man an instant before the dragon breathed fire from its maw.

I winced as I felt the heat, despite my fire charm earrings. Not only were they useful at protecting me from burns in my everyday work in the forge, I was proud of how I'd shaped them into cute anime style flame characters. But I wasn't sure they'd stand up to a direct dragon blast. I heaved myself to my feet as the dragon flew past. "Run!" I shouted at the soldier, who up close I realised was the same general who had started this mess.

We ran back to the shelter of the buildings as the dragon swept back and let loose more flames. The tarmac bubbled under the heat of its breath.

As I panted, hoping we were safe, the dragons' heads turned. They looked north, past the castle and Bute Park. They did a lap of the stadium and the female dropped low, snatching something in her large claws, before they all headed north, ignoring the sporadic explosions aimed at them.

The adrenaline left my body and I sank to the ground, leaning on a painted door. The paint had started to bubble from the heat of the battle and it caught on my frizzy hair. I saw Aloora and Dot marching towards us and I closed my eyes.

The general spoke into his walkie talkie in wonderment, "They've gone. Heading north, north west. We did it!"

A cheer went up from the straggling soldiers and the remaining protestors. Aloora scoffed, "You did nothing, except create this situation and I will be putting in a full report on this. We convinced the dragons to leave and you'd better respect them this time or I will be suggesting a parliamentary committee on your actions."

The general opened his mouth and blinked, not believing the gall of the gnome that barely came up to his chest. I smiled. I liked Aloora on the warpath. She turned to me. "And what were you thinking of running into the fight like that?! You could have been killed! Stop being a bloody hero!" Maybe I wasn't such a big fan of her warlike mood.

"Don't even worry about it, I'm fine," I replied weakly, "I couldn't let him be killed. Even if he did start this."

The general opened his mouth to protest then thought better of it and stalked away to take his annoyance out on someone else.

My friend huffed, but when she spoke, I knew I had won her over by blaming the general, "You're an idiot. Come on, let's get you home."

"Where did the dragons go?" I asked as they escorted me back to Royal Arcade.

Dot smiled, "The elves agreed they could settle over the Welsh hills. They've set up enchantments to hide local villages and farms so the dragons can fish or feast on the monsters that live near Breconia."

"The elven city? They're generous."

"They owe the Office some favours…and they love saving the day."

Guess I wasn't the only one who didn't have the highest opinion of the gorgeous magical creatures. With the dragons gone, I left arguing with the General to Aloora and Dot and headed home. I fell asleep as soon as my head hit the pillow.

Chapter 4

I woke sluggishly, my muscles still complaining from the exertion yesterday. I turned on my laptop and loaded up one of my superhero movies as pleasant undemanding background noise while I got dressed. I listened to the tell-tale patter of raindrops hitting the glass roof of the Arcade and sighed as I made myself a coffee. It wasn't as good as the brew from the Dragon's Head but it would have to do.

I made my way downstairs to my shop, laptop balanced on one hand, my favourite coffee mug in the other and plonked myself behind the shabby chic counter. I walked over the hardwood floor to unlock the door and tried to avoid staring at the massive mural that plastered one of the walls, but, as always, it drew my gaze.

An armoured female dwarf, complete with braided beard, gave me a saucy wink as she looked out onto the displays. She held an ornamental sword in an action pose next to graffiti style writing that proclaimed the name of my shop: Welcome to Amethyst's Treasures.

It contrasted starkly with the clean, modern, minimalist look I had envisaged for my shop but I couldn't remove it without hurting Marco's feelings. Annoyingly, it did draw people in and I was getting canny at converting selfies into sales.

I guessed the weather today and the chaos last night would put people off coming into the city. It was annoying how things conspired against honest business women. I wandered into my forge cum workshop in the back room and grabbed my jeweller's tools and the latest piece I was working on so I could craft whilst waiting for customers.

I had decided to turn the amethyst stone I was given in a new age shop in Avebury into a necklace. It offered me protection apparently so I figured I might as well keep it on me at all times. It was already polished so I didn't want to try to cut it, I liked the uneven smooth shape.

I had decided on a simple mount, but had been putting off completing it in favour of creating decorative swords for my young, usually male, clientele who liked to take pictures of themselves in front of the well-endowed female dwarf painted on the shop wall. They also liked shiny, fantasy weaponry and I liked taking their money.

I was carefully mounting it into a copper wire setting when I heard the shop bell tinkle merrily, indicating a customer had just entered. I looked up and plastered on my shopkeeper's smile, "Good morning and welcome to Amethyst's Treasures, I'm Amethyst, how may I help you today?"

My smile faltered a little as I took in the shopper. A dwarf, short even by dwarven standards was standing in the middle of the shop floor, looking around with a disinterested gaze at my wares. His grey beard was plaited neatly and hung past his belt. His hair was slicked back into a tidy ponytail, tied with a leather cord and he was wearing a smart, black suit. His eyes lingered on the large mural of the female dwarf and he almost let his calm composure slip as he gaped at it.

My eyes caught a small movement from outside the shop and I noticed the two dwarves that had taken up position either side of my glass door. They too were wearing suits, but they were also wearing dark glasses, despite the weather, and were holding large no nonsense pickaxes.

These weren't standard mining tools. They had large gleaming blades and an evil point on the other side. The guards were holding them in a manner that said "don't even think about it". My mind raced as I tried to think what the dwarf now studying me could want.

He stepped forward confidently and coughed to draw my attention, "Ms Amethyst Haernson, I presume."

I nodded, despite there being no question, "How may I help you, Mr…?"

"Master Ironfist," he took a card smoothly from his suit pocket and laid it in front of me, pushing it towards me. I took it and tried not to let my expression change as I recognised the crest, "member of the Dwarven Arms Council."

One of my Dad's sayings came to me: 'it never hurts to butter up members of the Council,' plus I had no idea what they wanted with me, "I'm honoured that you have chosen to visit my humble premises,"

The dwarf nodded with a tiny smile as if I had passed some sort of test I hadn't been aware of, "We have heard you are passing off your wares as dwarf-made…" he let the accusation hang in the air. This was serious, to try and pass myself off as a full dwarf craftswoman was anathema to the purity of the Council.

"No, no, not at all!" I protested.

He deliberately turned to look at the artwork plastered over one wall, "Hmmm…."

"It was a painting a friend did for me, that's all," my head was spinning.

He took out a smartphone in a neat black case emblazoned with the Council's logo of a hammer and an axe crossing over an anvil. Their motto curled below it in a fancy font I couldn't read. I knew it by heart anyway: Dwarv yn pûr - Dwarven is purity.

He tapped the screen a couple of times and held it up to me, showing pictures taken in my shop tagged #epicdwarf.

I swallowed hard, "I didn't realise I couldn't have a painting of myself on my wall, I'm not claiming to be a dwarf. It doesn't say it anywhere in the shop," I was warming to my theme, brazenly defending the picture I had hated a few short moments ago. I was also getting pissed off at the audacity of the Council who didn't even acknowledge half-breeds such as myself telling me how to decorate.

"Hmmm..." his murmur was more thoughtful this time.

I carried on, "It's not my fault if ignorant people get confused!" I stopped myself then, had I gone too far?

He nodded slightly with a smile, “No, we cannot hold you to account for other people’s ignorance.” I breathed a small sigh of relief as he turned towards the door. As he reached the handle, he turned back thoughtfully, “There is one more thing…”

I blinked as if I’d misheard him, had this smart dwarf just turned into a seventies detective? I had caught Columbo reruns as my Mum loved old crime shows, but I had never heard anyone say that in real life.

“…your axe…”

“My axe?” I repeated dumbly.

“May I see it?”

I weighed up my options: let him see it or piss him off and he would get his two guards-dwarves involved. I decided the first one was my best course of action and reluctantly removed Bane from its usual spot under my counter and laid it on the distressed wood.

He moved his hand over it reverently, showing respect for the master-crafted weapon. “This is a dwarven blade.”

I nodded, although again it hadn’t been phrased as a question.

“It is not seemly for such a blade to be with one such as you.”

“A shopkeeper you mean?” I said in a sugary sweet tone. I didn’t like where this was going but I wasn’t going to make it easy for him.

He had the decency to look a little uncomfortable as he shifted slightly in his polished, black hobnail boots, “One who is not fully a dwarf.”

I bristled at that and stood up from my chair, drawing myself up to my full height, which I was pleased to note was a few inches taller than the Council member. "That axe has been in my family for generations and was passed to me by my father, Dafydd Haernson, in the traditional coming of age ceremony. I have whetted the blade and polished the handle and spat on the earth in oath."

"Nevertheless…" he started.

"Wait a minute, you refuse to acknowledge me as a full dwarven mastercraftswoman despite my knowledge of the ancient smithing techniques, despite my Dad being a mastercraftsdwarf and one of your most knowledgeable teachers. Do you even have jurisdiction over what I can and can't do?" I borrowed the long, official sounding word I'd overheard Aloora use yesterday, "Over what I can and can't have?"

I realised my voice had raised as I let out a lot of pent up anger out in that speech. It wasn't fair! He shifted again and I realised he didn't actually have the power to take anything from me.

"I'll take that back, thank you," I calmly extended my hand, willing it not to tremble. He shot me a look of something like respect and handed me back my ancestral axe.

"I will need to see the proper documentation that your father has indeed passed the weapon to you and I will be checking into the weapon's history. Completion of the coming of age ceremony is insufficient as you are…not a full dwarf. Please send it into our Council e-mail address for verification to avoid another…visit."

I nodded, holding my axe across my chest. He turned and this time actually left, sweeping the guards-dwarves in his wake. Their hobnail boots clattered along the tiled floor, fading as he left the Arcade.

I allowed myself a few deep meditative breaths before putting Bane back in its usual place under the counter and calling Dad.

I stamped my feet and bit my lip nervously while I listened to the phone ring. After what felt like an eternity, he finally answered, "Hello?"

"Hi Dad, how's things?"

"Good, good, you know your mother. She's on a new organisation kick and keeps hiding the phone in a new place every day. I blame her friends, they're all into some Netflix series on cleaning."

My lips curled upwards at the thought of Mum reorganising the house again. It happened at least once a year and many of my treasured childhood possessions had been lost to her bouts of cleaning. I still wasn't one hundred per cent sure where my favourite teddy bear, Mr Baggins, had ended up.

"So, why are you calling during shop hours, love?" Typical Dad, always thinking with his business head on, "Do you want me to find your Mum? I think she's out in the garden…"

"Actually I wanted to talk to you," I took a deep breath, "I've just had a visit from the Dwarven Arms Council.

Dad swore, "Those stuffed shirts?! What did they want?"

“They don’t believe Bane is mine Dad, they were going to take it,” I stifled a sob by shoving my knuckles in my mouth.

There was a long pause, “You haven’t used it against another dwarf have you?”

“Dad!”

“Alright, alright, I had to check. You’ve been fighting dragons and such this past year, it’s not that farfetched,”

“I haven’t fought any dragons! I’ve cowered from them as they’ve tried to kill me!” I stopped protesting, maybe I had tried to fight at least one dragon this year.

“OK…well if you haven’t used it against another dwarf, outside of a formal combat challenge, of course, then they can’t take it off you unless they can prove you’ve stolen it.”

“Really?”

“Really, the Council only takes dwarfmade weapons back in extreme circumstances. If they’ve been used against dwarfkind or stolen,” I found myself nodding along. Weapons made by dwarves for non-dwarves were technically on loan and could be reclaimed if they were misused, which generally meant killing dwarves.

“Who was it who came to see you?”

I picked up the business card from the counter where I had left it, “Master B Ironfist,” I read out.

“Right, well I’ll be making some calls to the Council about this, you can be sure!”

“Thanks Dad, can you send in the paperwork too?” I was confident Dad had made the right legal documents when he passed the axe on to me, dwarves were a bit obsessive about that sort of thing.

“Of course, of course, we’ll get this sorted out. How’s Marco doing? He did a great job with the painting didn’t he? Really dwarfed up the place I thought.” Dad had been a co-conspirator in the summer when Marco had decided to redecorate my shop and had been on board with the mural from the start.

“It’s growing on me,” I replied, gazing at the picture as I heard Mum call something in the background.

“Right, well, you’d better get back to work, hey? Your Mum says to say hi to you and she wants to meet your elf boyfriend. Got to go, love, bye.” He hung up as I was protesting strongly that nothing was going on. Mum was fixated on the picture of Lorandir and I that had appeared in a Cardiff paper after the first dragon had been awakened and kept making inappropriate comments about me and the elf being in a relationship. I chewed my lip as I thought about it. We had shared a kiss in a weird post-apocalyptic moment after the red dragon had been woken by a cult, but since then we had been nothing more than friendly.

I shook my head and refilled my cup of coffee before settling back again on my seat. Now I was thinking more clearly, I was getting more and more annoyed about the visit from the Council. I twisted the copper wire on my counter energetically, turning my frustration into productivity.

I finished the twist and stood back, studying the deep purple stone in its new setting. I had chosen copper to amplify the power in the amethyst and the metal set off the dark colour perfectly. I was so lost in its beauty that I almost missed my first customer of the day.

She coughed politely to get my attention and I slipped into my shopkeeper's persona instantly. The wealthy older lady was interested in a bracelet for her granddaughter and eventually settled on a beaten silver cuff with a large white opal set into it.

The rest of the day was so quiet that, after I'd finished my necklace, I slipped out to Gundersson's Dwarfish Delicatessen next to my shop for a snack. His prices were high, but I felt in need of a little comfort food after my encounter this morning.

As I walked the short distance back to my shop, I noticed a hooded figure running along the Arcade carrying a spray can. I tutted and didn't think much of it until I saw my shop window. Someone, and I made a wild leap that it was the hoody I had seen legging it, had scrawled across the glass:

Free the Dragons

Brilliant. I chewed mournfully on the dried sausage I had bought, took a picture on my phone and went inside. What did it even mean? It could be related to the cult I had tangled with earlier in the year or one of the activists who always wanted to put wyrms on the registered species list so they couldn't be household pets. There was too much to think about. Sighing and finishing my snack, I filled a bucket with warm soapy water and began cleaning it off.

The scant amount of shoppers shot me sympathetic looks as I scrubbed.

Chapter 5

I was washing off the last 's' when Marco and Aloora turned up for our usual games night. I had forgotten about it with all the excitement of a visit from the Council and the vandalism of my window.

"What 'appened?" Marco looked aghast at the dirty wet cloths piled up beside me and my soaking clothes.

"Some miscreant sprayed paint all over my shop, culs." I swore in Dwarfish, "Do you know what 'Free the Dragons' means?"

Aloora shook her head and handed me a familiar paper cup from the Dragon's Head, "New one on me, but I'll keep my ear to the ground for you. Are we still on for tonight?"

I nodded and thanked her for the sweet syrupy coffee and for looking into the mysterious slogan. With her social media contacts and her job at the Magical Liaison Office, I was sure she'd find out if it meant anything. I heaved the plastic bucket of dirty water inside. I'd finish the remaining half letter tomorrow morning before the Arcade opened.

My friends traipsed up the wooden stairs to my living space ahead of me and began perusing my games collection. They filled what shelf space I had, alongside my fantasy fiction novels. The dangers of living close to both a board games shop and a book store.

While they selected a game, I dried myself and got changed into a comfy superhero hoody and some new jeans. Errol trotted upstairs and wrapped himself around Aloora's legs. She smiled and obliged him with some of the beef jerky she always kept in her leather satchel for him. She made him sit up and beg like a dog for the next piece while Marco set up a game of Ticket to Ride. My table was a little small for it, but we crowded round and only a couple of corners hung over the edge of the sanded wooden top.

I brought two beers and a vodka coke for me to the table to sit alongside the hot drinks and nearly cried with joy when I saw Aloora unwrap a bag of brownies I hadn't noticed she was carrying.

"Are those Brinda's brownies?" I licked my lips in anticipation at the Dragon's Head own recipe brownies.

Aloora nodded and passed one over. "Nice necklace!" she grabbed it as I bent to reach the proffered cake, studying it, "It suits you,"

"Thanks, it's the jewel I got I Avebury," I sank down onto my second hand sage green armchair and demolished the brownie in three bites. I loved those things. I put on some soft rock music on my laptop for background noise while we started to play.

I was just connecting a route on the board from Los Angeles to New York while Marco talked about his new job in set design for one of the theatre houses, when I heard a noise downstairs. A strange cracking sound. The others heard it too and turned in their seats. I frowned and made my way downstairs. Half way down the wooden steps, I noticed the flames burning merrily in the centre of the shop floor.

A broken bottle lay in the midst of the flames and the fire was spreading quickly. "Got your flame charms?" I asked quickly. They nodded. Aloora tapped her earrings, the mirror of mine and Marco grabbed his keyring. "We've got to move!"

I shoved my feet into my sturdy leather boots in case there was broken glass over the floor and led the way, grabbing Errol and rushing through the fire. He looked as if he was enjoying the warmth but I didn't like how the flames were spreading. I shoved Errol into Aloora's arms while Marco called the emergency services. I had to go back in. I heard a shout as they realised what I was doing but my whole life was in there.

My fire charm protected me from burning but it wasn't exactly a comfortable heat. I waded through the fire to recover Bane from under the counter then into the coolness of my forge to grab the tools my Dad had gifted me. It took two trips to get everything and I grabbed my red leather jacket on the way back out, draping it over my shoulders. I was weighing up whether to go back in for my jewellery collections or try to get back upstairs and grab some clothes when Marco grabbed me, "Don't go back in!" he shouted over the roar of the blaze that had taken hold, "It is not safe!"

As if to emphasise his words, the shop ceiling began to sag and a piece fell onto the countertop with a bang. The paint on the mural began to curl and the dwarf started to turn black before the paint bubbled and peeled away.

I heard the welcome sounds of sirens. The fire brigade arrived and efficiently dealt with the blaze. They bagged up the remains of the firebomb and contacted the police to report an arson attack. The officers arrived and took statements, asking me if I had any enemies, if I knew who had done it. To their credit, their eyebrows didn't raise too much as I listed cult members, the Dwarven Arms Council and wyrm rights activists.

We headed back to Aloora and Marco's house share, carrying my tools and axe between us. The streetlights glowed in the slow drizzle as we trudged across the city. It was the sort of rain that soaked through to the skin and Errol shifted uncomfortably on my shoulders.

Once we stepped inside the old but dry Victorian house, Aloora found me some blankets and I set up a makeshift bed on the sofa. I had hoped that some of their less than friendly housemates might have left the city in fear of the dragons, but no such luck. Marco leant me a pair of flannel pyjamas as my clothes were both soot stained and soaking. They were snug around my chest and far too long for me, but they were warm and dry so I thanked him and settled down to try to sleep. Errol curled up next to me, a welcome hot water bottle against the draughty room. I lay awake for a long time with silent tears leaking down my face.

The next morning, I was awakened by the sounds of students showering and grabbing breakfast. One of the house mates came into the lounge, saw me, gave an exasperated sigh and left again. My phone rang and I glanced at the time before I answered it. Nine o'clock. Why did it feel later?

I answered the phone with a croaky voice, "Hello Mr. Davies,"

"Morning there Amethyst, sorry to hear about your shop see," the owner of the Arcade was sympathetic.

"Have you had to shut down the Arcade?" my voice was small.

"No, no trouble there, the fire brigade put it out quick enough, there's no damage to any of the other units. I've got everyone asking if you're alright though,"

"Yeah, don't even worry about it, I'm fine. Me and Errol got out."

"I'm glad to hear that, so I am. I wanted to say that my insurance will cover the structural repairs but not contents of course, so you sort that out with your own company. I'll send you over the details if the firms need to talk to each other, see.

"And I've cordoned it off so if you want to come back round and collect anything, you do that. Gundersson's keeping an eye on the place so no one will get in until you've been back. Is there anything you need there?"

My mind listed all the things I now didn't have: clothes, proper bedding, wyrm food for Errol, a place to call home. I answered, "No, no I'm fine, like I said don't even worry about it. I'll pop by the shop later."

"Right-o then, cheerio."

I lifted a sofa cushion over my face and screamed into it, muffling my frustration.

Chapter 6

After letting out my anger, I called the insurance company and registered my claim for the shop contents and the rent. As my living arrangements were less than official, I couldn't exactly claim for my personal things that had perished in the blaze.

I thought longingly of my wizard-shaped lamp, my comfy sage green armchair and my laptop filled with superhero movies. The lady on the other end of the phone gave me an email address, asked for a stock list and previous rental invoices to be sent through and promised me she would process the claim as quickly as she could. After making the call, I felt drained and in need of sustenance.

I snuck into Aloora's room. My friend was not a morning person and I didn't want to be the one to wake her. I grabbed a belt and made a makeshift lead for Errol. After a moment's thought, I grabbed a backpack as well and left a quick note that I'd gone out.

I set a brisk pace as I stormed across town, working out my emotions as I walked. I'm pretty sure I was muttering to myself by the time I made it to the Dragon's Head café. Thankful for instant payments via smartphones, I bought myself some much needed caffeine and a bacon sandwich.

Brinda gave me a look as I inhaled the sweet scent of coffee before taking a long drink. I was puzzled until I looked down and realised I was still in my borrowed pyjamas. I shrugged, not trusting myself to speak without crying. She smiled at me and shook her head in a motherly sort of way. I smiled back, gave half of my sandwich to Errol and we left.

I slowed as I got closer to the Arcade, steeling myself to go in and see the desolation of my life in person. I decided to delay the inevitable and called Mum and Dad to let them know I was OK.

Mum picked up immediately, "Hello?"

"Hi Mum,"

"Ame! Lovely to hear from you, I was just thinking I needed to come to the big city and see my little girl, and do some shopping,"

I grimaced, "Actually, I might need to do a bit of shopping myself…"

"Lovely, I always thought you needed to update your wardrobe…"

I interrupted quickly before she got too caught up in the mother-daughter shopping fantasy she enjoyed but which always felt more like torture to me, "I meant I've lost everything…there was a fire…" I choked then and started crying.

Passers-by looked on with alarm to see such a brazen display of public emotion. I ignored them.

"Oh, Ame, are you OK?"

"Yeah, yeah, Errol and I got out, but everything else Mum, it's gone."

"Oh love, I'll come and get you, you stay with us. Now tell me exactly where you are."

"It's ok Mum, I'm staying with Aloora and Marco for now. I need to be here to sort out the insurance and the police…"

"Police?! What happened?"

I regretted mentioning that detail now so bluffed my way out, "It's nothing Mum, just standard procedure."

I could tell from the silence that Mum wasn't buying it, she watched enough crime shows that she knew more about standard procedure than I did. I heard her call for my Dad and tell him that my livelihood had burned down and he needed to talk some sense into me.

"Amethyst? What's this your mother's told me about your shop?"

"She's right, it's burned down. Don't worry, Errol and I got out and I managed to save my tools, and Bane. I'm going there now to see if I can recover anything else."

"And you were insured?" Typical Dad, straight down to business.

"Yep, I've already called them. I need to email over some documents but it's fine."

"And you have somewhere to stay?"

I confirmed that I did.

"And do you want to come and stay with us?"

"No thanks Dad, I need to stay here, try to speed things up with the insurance so I can get back on my feet quickly."

He gave a gruff acknowledgement of my stubbornness, "Alright then, well the offer's there if you want it. Just call and we'll pick you up. Anytime. I'll handle your mother."

"Thanks Dad, love you both." I hung up, grateful that he understood.

Wiping the tears from my face, I squared my shoulders and entered the Arcade. I ignored the sympathetic looks from other shopkeepers but Gundersson came out from his deli to clap me on the back and offer to help.

I thanked him then shook my head and told him I was only here to see what I could salvage. He nodded and returned to his shop.

I took a deep breath and then looked up at my own premises. It was a dismal sight. My sleek shop sign was undamaged, proclaiming 'Amethyst's Treasures' in modern lettering. Beneath it, the door was hanging off its hinges and the shop window was smashed. Shards jutted upwards menacingly. I stepped over the threshold.

Errol bounded to the back room in search of coal and I heard him munching noisily. I looked around. Part of the ceiling had caved in and lay smashed on the floor amongst shards of glass from my display cabinets. I almost felt sorry for the painted dwarf as half her face had been burned off and the lettering next to her now spelled 'We com A y s T eas es' in less vibrant colours.

The stairs were blackened but intact. I tested my weight on one then another until I could peek upstairs. There was obviously a large hole where the floor had fallen through and the walls were a strange sooty grey colour. I risked stepping onto the wooden floor. It squealed ominously at my weight and I noticed water seeping around my boot. Of course everything would be waterlogged.

I decided to try to grab some clothes at least and cautiously tiptoed around the opening in the floor to my small wardrobe. As I suspected, everything was soaking so I grabbed a handful of t-shirts and jeans and turned to go back. As I did, I spotted the unharmed mucklewhite mushrooms behind the sink in my kitchen. The only plant I had managed to keep alive and a dwarven delicacy. I tiptoed over lightly and added their pot to my pile. As I was making my way back to the staircase, my sturdy boots slipped on the wet floor and I landed hard on my bottom. Wincing, I tried to stand, "Well that was luck…"

The floor beneath me collapsed and I fell in a heap of wood and clothes to the shop floor below with a loud crash. "..y" I wheezed. The mushrooms in their pot rolled away from me, still unhurt in the fall. The absurdity of it all made me start to laugh hysterically.

I didn't hear anything until a familiar voice beside me asked, "Are you OK Ame?" I felt a hand on my shoulder and I turned, trying to breathe instead of laugh. I looked into the familiar green eyes of Lorandir who was crouching next to me in the debris and something released in my chest. I shook my head and my shoulders shook as my laughter turned into heaving sobs.

He wrapped his arms around me and held me as I let it all out in keening moans. When I was done, I pulled away, embarrassed.

"Sorry about that."

He looked at me as if I was crazy. I was sitting in the middle of a wreckage, wearing pyjamas whilst crying so he probably had a point, but he simply said, "Don't apologise. How can I help?"

I looked around, "I came to see if I could salvage anything but upstairs is too dangerous." I rubbed my face with the back of my hand, "I haven't checked the back room…Errol!" I got up in a sudden panic that my pet wyrm had come to danger while I had been messing around. I stepped around fallen wood to get to the door of my forge and sighed.

Errol was still eating his coal and actually the backroom didn't look too bad. My workbench was still intact. Even the small kettle and cups had survived, "Tea?" I asked instinctively.

Lorandir furrowed his brow and shook his head. I tried the kettle. It didn't work. Of course all the water would have damaged the electrics. I was such a moron. I pushed my hair out of my eyes and noticed my enchanting goggles dangling on one end of the work bench. I'd missed them last night and I shoved them on my head. The dark brown lenses allowed me to see the enchantments I worked into my jewellery and I'd had them custom made so was glad to rescue them. I grabbed my favourite mug, with a dragon that looked a bit like Errol printed on it and shoved it into the backpack. Then I went to get the clothes. They were dripping wet.

"You can't take them," the elf was practical.

"It's these or pyjamas," I shrugged.

He shook his head, "I'll buy you new ones just please don't take them."

I looked anew at the sodden pile of clothes, now covered in ash from the floor where I'd left them. I picked out my favourite red leather jacket and left the rest. Maybe he was right but I had my pride. "I can buy my own clothes!"

"What else?" he was helping me think and I was grateful.

"Er, see if there's any stock I can take," I looked around the broken display cases and wandered over. Silver had melted, the fire must have been hot. The ornamental swords that hung on the wall were blackened. I shoved them in the bag too. I pulled the goggles over my eyes, searching for any enchanted jewellery that wasn't obvious. A few fire charms had survived but the heat of the blaze had melted most of the jewellery and destroyed any enchantments I'd placed on them as the objects twisted shape in the heat.

A golden glow came from near the counter, it wasn't my magic and I scrabbled around to try and locate the source. There, undamaged, was the dragon scale I had found in the tunnel that connected Avebury and Stonehenge. I put it thoughtfully in my backpack. It contained powerful magic and I wondered if I'd be able to meld mine with it.

I sighed. If only I could create unlosable jewellery then I might be able to find more of my stock. I'd been toying with the idea ever since I had seen Espretha's pendant that

Lorandir had used to find her in the spring. But I hadn't been able to come up with any ideas to replicate the elven enchantment that tied metal to magical signatures. I scuffed the debris with my boot and found a bracelet. I retrieved it from the rubble and placed it in the backpack. I cradled the pot of mushrooms under one arm then called Errol to me.

"At least the mural you hated is gone," Lorandir commented as we left, his arm around my shoulders, supporting me.

"It was starting to grow on me," I burst into laughter again.

Gundersson called after me as I left. I turned slowly and saw him carrying a large cardboard box, "A few bits from your friends at the Arcade." I opened my mouth to protest but he pressed the box of goodies into my hands and turned on his heels before I could hand it back to him.

I looked down and smiled as I saw my favourite dried sausages and a couple of cakes from the café in the Arcade. I was a simple creature at heart.

"Shopping or food first?" Lorandir asked.

I looked down at Marco's pyjamas, now soiled and sodden and clinging to me uncomfortably. "Clothes." I led the way to a nearby shop that sold printed t-shirts, hoodies and jeans and picked out a small selection. I left looking and feeling a lot better.

Lorandir steered me to The Rummer for food and I savoured the steak and chips, splashing out on peppercorn sauce to accompany it. The elf did most of the talking while I tucked in, Errol curled up at my feet. I had the impression he was trying to distract me and I was enjoying hearing about the elven city of Breconia and his childhood there, it was working. Then he ordered two of their chocolate fudge cakes and I moaned in pleasure as I ate it slowly.

Feeling a lot more like my normal self, he insisted on carrying the care package and walking me back to the house share. "If it gets too crowded, you could come stay with me. I'll always have a bed for you," he offered. I started to blush and my mouth opened and closed before he added, "in your own room, I mean…I have a spare room."

I almost laughed. Of course that was what he meant. I was such an idiot, "Where do you live when you're in Cardiff?" I was curious.

"My family got a place in the Bay where I can stay since I'm spending so much time here now on their business."

I was about to follow up on that, since I wasn't entirely sure what he did for a living, when my phone rang. I checked the caller ID and answered, "Hi Gunther,"

"Amethyst! Your father told me what happened, why didn't you call?" A close friend of my father, Gunther was also my supplier and could get his hands on anything.

"I didn't know how to break it to you, I don't know if I'll have any more orders for you for a while."

He made a scoffing noise, "Don't worry about that. Aloora said it was an attack."

It was amazing how quickly news could spread, "It was, but I have no idea who."

“I’m putting my kobold security team on it, they keep their pointed ears close to the ground. If I find anything out, I’ll let you know.”

“Thanks Gunther, you’re a good friend.”

He brushed off the compliment, “Well I need my best customer able to run her business unafraid! Call me if you need anything.”

I shook my head at the phone as he hung up. “You have good friends,” Lorandir commented a little forlornly. As I was getting to know the elf, I was realising that his cocksure exterior was a cover. He was still hurting from the loss of his best friend to a cult. The same friend who was giving me covert sparring lessons.

I opened my mouth to tell him when he gripped my shoulder and pulled me back. I stumbled into him, about to shout when I noticed the bright red tour bus whizz past, its horn honking loudly. I had been so caught up in my own thoughts, I had nearly stepped onto a busy street. He held me tightly and murmured, “Are you ok?” against my thick hair.

I nodded mutely, unable to process the sudden heat I was feeling pressed up against his muscular body, the box of goodies digging into my side. The glazed pot of Mucklewhite mushrooms slipped and bounced onto the pavement. He held me for another second longer than necessary then released me. All thoughts of Espretha left my mind.

Chapter 7

After retrieving the mushrooms, we walked back the rest of the way in silence. I had forgotten a key and didn't want to break in with my own key that allowed me to circumvent most locks. It felt wrong to do it to a friend's house, so I knocked loudly as we stood on the tiled Victorian porch, black bin bags piled up in the small front garden and across the street. I had forgotten how scummy student housing could be, and round here it was all student housing.

I moved from the door to the window of Aloora's ground floor room and knocked again. This time I heard movement and a few moments later, my gnomish friend opened the door. She clocked Lorandir and gave me a knowing smile before ushering us both in to her room. Errol tagged along and immediately found the warmest spot by the radiator.

"Well, did you save anything?"

I put the shopping bags containing my new clothes and Marco's pyjamas on the floor and upended the backpack onto her bed, sending weapons, jewellery and my mug sprawling across her duvet cover. My red jacket made a squelching sound as it hit the covers. She curled her lip. I hastily removed it and stood there while it dripped damply onto the floor.

She hurried to remove a pile of paperwork from the splash zone and waved me to the bathroom, "Hang it over the bath until it's dry!"

I complied meekly before she forced me to bin it. When I returned, she was plying Lorandir with questions about Elvish past participles in magical language. He looked thoroughly confused and I turned my snort of laughter into a cough.

"Sorry Ally, I just speak the language," he managed, his long hands held upright to pacify her.

She huffed and turned back to her open laptop, tapping away furiously on the keys. Lorandir opened his mouth to say something but I caught his eye and shook my head warningly. If we distracted her now, she'd only get upset. She finished her paragraph with a flourish and did a celebratory twirl on her swivel seat.

"OK," she smiled, "what shall we have to eat tonight. Takeout's on me. I fancy Chinese."

I nodded along, "Can we play a game first? We've had a massive meal at The Rummer."

Aloora looked at me knowingly, "Sure thing, Ghostel?" she named one of our favourite games to play, rubbing her hands in anticipation. She always won.

Lorandir stood and deposited the cardboard box he'd been cradling onto Aloora's bed next to the sorry remains of my shop, "I'd love to, but I have to go."

"What?" This was news to me, "Why? I mean…"

He gave me a lopsided smile, "I came to the shop to tell you I'd be out of town for a while. The dragons moved to the countryside outside Breconia a couple of nights ago and my family want me back with them. They seem to think I'm an expert because I've been present when they were freed."

I knew that feeling. Being thought of as an expert because you've happened to witness a dragon awakening was the reason we had both been present for the second and third dragons' awakenings at the Summer Solstice.

He walked out of the room and I followed, "Thanks, er, for today I mean, I don't know what I'd have done without you with me." I meant it.

There was that lopsided smile again, "No problem," he struggled with the door for a second before turning to me with a confused expression.

I smiled and stepped forward, "You have to jiggle it," I demonstrated, wiggling the handle up and down until it finally opened. I turned back to him, suddenly aware of how close we were in the narrow hallway. He tucked a tendril of hair behind my ear and lifted my chin slightly. I bit my lip nervously. He sighed and pulled me into a hug.

"I'll see you soon, mellon canya nin, galad'Amethysta," he breathed into my ear, the Elvish language sounding like a caress. I watched him walk down the street, still shining from yesterday's rain before I shut the door and leaned back against the chipped wallpaper lining the hall.

What was that and what did it mean? I thought of asking Aloora, she spoke Elvish, as well as Draconic and about five other languages, but part of me wanted to keep it to myself, imagining what it might mean. I didn't mention it when I joined Aloora in her room. She was back at her laptop, engrossed in whatever research she was doing.

"How did your steamy goodbye go?"

I mumbled something and she laughed, only half listening.

I settled onto her bed and picked up one of her books. They were almost all academic, but being about dragons, some of them were quite interesting to read. This one was bound in green leather and gold lettering spelled out *A Discourse on Dragon Breeding*. It didn't have the most promising title but managed to engross me as the author used fossilised remains and ancient texts to consider whether dragons could be bred and how they cared for their young. Apparently they looked after them well into adolescence. I thought of the smaller white dragon and wondered if that was considered a teenager even though it was almost as long as a city bus.

Chapter 8

The next morning, Aloora bounded into the lounge I had adopted as my room just as the sun was starting to peek through the gap in the ill-fitting curtains.

She sat on the sagging sofa and prodded me awake, "Wha? You're never up early! Leave me be gnome!"

She bounced up and down instead, "I'm readjusting my body clock now I've got to do some work in office hours for the MLO,"

I groaned and rolled over, "I don't think I like the impact corporate life is having on you,"

Aloora laughed, "Well get used to it, we've got an assignment!"

"What?" I couldn't process cryptic clues this early in the morning without caffeine. My friend was ahead of me as she pressed a hot cup of instant coffee into my hands and pulled me to a sitting position.

"You're coming into the office with me! The dragons are behaving weirdly and they want some experts. You're not doing anything and you've got more first-hand experience with the creatures than almost anyone, you can come too."

"Don't wanna," I whinged childishly and gestured at the communal TV set in the corner of the room, "I've got to catch up on my daytime TV."

Aloora gave me a look, "It could get you back on your feet faster. I'll pay you," I narrowed my eyes at my friend, "I mean the Office often takes on contractors, come on, it beats watching a hundred ways to style your eyebrows on the telly!"

"Fine," I gave in as Aloora opened her mouth to keep protesting. It wasn't like I had anything better to do and it would be nice to earn some money instead of just waiting for the insurance payout. I groaned, I'd forgotten to send in the documents. I jotted a note in my phone to remind me to do it later.

I took a quick shower and got dressed in my new clothes. I wished I'd bought some new underwear too, but that had been far too embarrassing to contemplate with Lorandir in tow. I'd have to make time to do that today.

I took Errol with me, guessing the Magical Liaison Office would be open minded to my pet, and fell into step with Aloora, who was typing social media updates as she walked. She allowed me to stop off at the Dragon's Head to get a cup of proper coffee and some breakfast: a sausage bap smothered with ketchup, but insisted I got it to go. Brinda had heard what had happened to my shop and was sympathetic. I nodded, trying not to think about it. When I reached into the paper bag for my roll, I saw she'd put in one of her brownies free of charge. I felt a wave of love for that woman.

I was licking the last of the ketchup from my fingers when Aloora stopped outside of a non-descript door on a side road outside of the city centre. The black paint looked new and a small, discreet brass plaque read: Magical Liaison Office. If Aloora hadn't had been here, I wouldn't have looked twice. The door was sandwiched between a four-storey grey house that had been converted into offices and a run-down church with several holes where panes of glass once stood. I was distinctly unimpressed.

Aloora held up her pass to the brass plaque and something beeped and buzzed before the door opened inwards. She raised an eyebrow and walked in. I followed. Inside was a lot more modern than I was expecting. My sturdy boots echoed on the shiny tiled floor. Abstract paintings were hung along the walls. Aloora led us past several closed doors, all with key card locks on them. I chewed my lip as I tried to work out the architecture. From the outside, there didn't seem to be enough space for all the rooms we were passing.

My friend stopped abruptly in front of a maroon coloured wooden door, this one didn't have a key card and instead had a brass door knocker in the shape of a face. Whoever had made it had taken care to make it both lifelike and ugly. The ears were too large and were oddly asymmetrical and its mouth was turned down in a frown with deep, creased wrinkles either side of it.

Aloora held her pass up to it then sighed.

“Wake up Fred!” she lifted the brass ring that was attached to its upturned nose and rapped it twice on the wooden door.

My jaw dropped as the door knocker opened its eyes and spoke, “Alright, alright! Keep your hair on Miss! What do you want?”

“To get in!” Aloora rolled her eyes.

“Manners don’t cost anything you know,” Fred grumbled.

“Please will you let us in?”

“Where’s your pass?” My friend held up her pass again and Fred made an act of studying it closely. Then he saw me, “And who do we have here then?”

“She’s with me, taskforce assignment.”

Fred narrowed his eyes at me and for a second, I could have sworn that they glowed red. “Alright, but you’ll need to get her a pass made if she’s coming in again.” With that, the door swung open and she stepped through. I followed quickly, calling Errol to my side, in case Fred changed his mind.

I was about to ask Aloora about the door knocker but I was immediately distracted by the room we had just walked into. It was shaped like a pentagon, but with strange angles that didn’t quite add up. The door we had just entered by was set close to one of the corners and a large television set took up most of the rest of that wall.

Bookshelves lined three of the walls, stacked with huge leather-bound volumes. Several were almost the same height as me. An ancient carpet covered the floor, giving it the feel of a library in an old stately home. The fourth wall was comprised of an enormous fireplace, where flames burned fiercely and by all rights the room should have been as hot as an oven. Instead it was pleasantly warm. Errol immediately curled up as close to the fire as he could.

Above the fireplace hung an armoury of ancient weapons. I could sense the magical auras coming from several of them and wished I'd brought my goggles with me so I could get a better idea of the sorts of enchantments they held.

Aloora walked past the squashy leather sofas set up by the fireplace and headed for a small wooden desk that held a computer and a green angle poise lamp. She turned it on and pummelled the keyboard as she typed. I followed her and didn't bother to hide my amazement as I turned and looked around again.

I noticed Dot standing in front of one of the bookcases and said hello with a slight frown. She was stirring a cup of something hot with a silver spoon.

"Takes a bit of getting used to, doesn't it?" she smiled, "Fancy a drink? Kitchen's through there."

I shook my head, holding up my own cup of coffee. Then my brain caught up with her words. I looked behind her, where she had pointed. There was no door at all. I frowned and walked closer.

She laughed and pulled out a book. Immediately, a small section of a bookcase swung open. A secret door! My estimation of the Magical Liaison Office went up. I stepped through into a modern kitchen, neat cupboards lined the walls and there was even a small oven and grill. There was another door labelled 'WC' beyond that. I snagged a jammy dodger from an open packet left on the side and stepped back into the room. Dot pushed the book back into place. The panel slid shut behind me.

"Cool," I breathed in amazement as I bent to take a closer look at the black clothbound book, *Nom-Nomenclature of Supernatural Cuisine*. I almost winced at the bad pun.

Aloora had worked some magic with her laptop and there were now a series of videos streaming on the huge television set. She stood and walked closer, tilting her head as she studied the footage. Dot and I moved to stand beside her. The videos were blurry at best, taken by hikers in the Welsh mountains, who were incapable of holding their cameras still. The last video had a *Blair Witch* effect as it alternated shots of the dragons swooping overhead and roaring with running feet and, at one point, a hiker huddled under a tree breathing heavily while snot dripped down her face.

"What's going on Ally?"

My friend frowned, "I'm not sure. I'd have thought the new territory on the reservation would be perfect for them, but the dragons seem really agitated. A lot more so than when they were nesting in the Millennium Stadium."

Agent Jones' face suddenly appeared on the screen. Her amber eyes were as piercing as ever but her dark bob looked like it was growing out a little. I was surprised, I had never seen her look anything other than neat. Her break must be agreeing with her.

"Good morning everyone, I think we can agree we have a situation here. You've studied the footage. The elves are starting to push back on their offer to house the dragons in their territories and we need to resolve this before the politicians get involved again." Agent Jones spat the word politicians with the same venom I reserved for sugar-free cola.

"What do you recommend?" I was surprised that Dot was deferring to Aloora. The vampire had been part of the Magical Liaison Office for longer than my friend.

"I'd suggest a reconnaissance mission. I need to get closer to understand their behaviour better and we might pick up some more clues that the hikers missed, after all they were fleeing in fear of their lives." I was impressed. Aloora was fitting right in.

Agent Jones nodded. "Right."

"I'd also suggest a communications expert. Maxi helped me with the recordings from Cardiff, it would help to have his equipment along too."

Agent Jones' eyes narrowed, and I could have sworn that her pupils changed to slits at Maxi's name. I wondered if she'd shift into a lynx on the call. Maxi had been responsible for faulty communication equipment that had awoken the two dragons at Stonehenge during the Summer Solstice party. She shook her head, "Maxi is on another assignment, we'll have to make do without him. I'm sure the equipment we have onsite will be sufficient. I'll meet you at the entrance to the reserve at sixteen hundred hours sharp. Bring standard kit, and sign the dwarf on if she wants to be paid. Haernson, bring your axe." Agent Jones' face disappeared, leaving a white dot in the middle of the screen. I was blinking at the orders. Aloora was beaming at the thought of getting close to her beloved dragons again.

I sighed, “It’s a shame, I liked Maxi.”

Dot’s eyes narrowed this time and started to glow a dark red, “He let us all down earlier this year, tensions are still high between him and the boss, despite Aloora’s efforts to get them to kiss and make up.”

Aloora shrugged, nonplussed at the accusation, “He was misguided.”

“Even if I believed that, and I want to, he chose to mislead us when we needed him most,” Dot’s voice was shaking and I got the impression they were going over old ground. I tried to change the subject before it got any more awkward.

“What’s standard kit?” I asked dumbly.

Dot took a long swig from her mug. The glow in her eyes faded and they returned to their usual colour, which now I noticed it, was still red but more of a rusty colour that could pass for brown. She grabbed a black bag from under a desk and unzipped it. I looked inside. There were crossbows, bolts, knives and even a Taser. There was a set of spare clothes and, on top of these, were several balls of wool and a pair of wooden knitting needles. I gave the vampire an incredulous look and was rewarded with a toothy grin, “These reconnaissance missions are mostly waiting around; I like to keep busy. Would you like me to make you a scarf?”

I took a look at the rainbow coloured wool in the bag, not really my style, “I’m OK thanks. Er, what’s the other part of reconnaissance missions?”

Her smile widened and she licked her lips slowly, “Chasing down the bad guys.”

I gulped. Aloora patted me on the back, "Dragons aren't bad, they're just dragons. We'll have a look, try to get to the bottom of their erratic behaviour and be home before you know it…pack an overnight bag though, just in case."

"Er, I have to do a bit of shopping anyway. What time is sixteen hundred hours and when are we leaving here?"

Aloora laughed, "If you're going to work with us, you should really get a grip on military time. Agent Jones loves it. That's four o'clock to you and we'll need to be on the road by three. Are you going to be OK on your own for a bit?"

I nodded then a thought struck me, "What about Errol? I can't leave him with Marco, that's not fair, he's got his new job to think about and I don't think the producers of the latest Welsh musical will want a wyrm on set."

My friend screwed up her face, "He could come with us?"

I wasn't sure, he'd been through a lot. After all he'd lost his home in the fire too and I wasn't sure he'd enjoy being around large dragons acting aggressively. It would be ideal if there was a kennel for wyrms somewhere, like my Uncle Owain's wyrm farm. That idea gave me pause. He was based not far from Breconia…

"Could we make a stop on the way?"

Chapter 9

Despite the lighter foot traffic than usual in the city centre thanks to the recent riot, it was a depressing shopping trip, where I remembered too late that there was a reason I rarely bought myself underwear. Most shops didn't stock my size and whilst I desperately looked at fancy lacy numbers with exotic names, it was only ever plain bras with unattractive names that fit me. One of the hefty underwired concoctions might has well have been called *The Two Towers* – it had all the charm and engineering support of medieval architecture. I had thought that the few training sessions I had had with Espretha were tightening my curves, but the harsh lighting in the changing rooms stripped me of any feelings of sexiness as I hastily hooked on ill-fitting bras until I found one that vaguely fit.

I was so miserable that I didn't even fancy one of Brinda's cakes to cheer me up; I was only thinking of the inches it would add to my waist. I hated clothes shopping. I trudged back to Aloora's with Errol in tow, his nostrils smoking unhappily in the damp weather.

Once there, I dug into the care package with gusto as I packed a backpack with a change of clothes and my goggles. I shoved some dragon treats and Errol's lead into another bag that I scavenged from the kitchen, after checking that Aloora's housemates weren't in there. Then I turned on the television set and settled down to wait for the Magical Liaison Office to pick me up for my second assignment with them.

The TV seemed to be stuck on a channel that showed interior design shows back to back. I twirled the dragon scale I had found between my fingers, enjoying the smooth, warm feel of it in my hand as I watched. With my other hand, I shovelled the final cupcake into my mouth. By the time I heard a van pull up outside, I had learned more than I ever wanted to about chalk paint and silky finishes, and, to my horror, I had almost entirely finished the cardboard box of food.

Aloora was practically bouncing up and down in her seat as I hefted my bags and Errol into a familiar grey van. My friend was in the driving seat and epic fantasy music was blaring from the radio. I scuffed at the fire rune I had managed to etch into the van's floor when we had been fighting to escape tarfangtulas outside Stonehenge.

I noticed that the van had been made more comfy on the inside. Woollen throws covered the seats in rainbow colours. Bags were placed into webbed storage baskets to keep them secure, in case of more supernatural attacks. My eyes lingered on the weapons strapped safely to the metal walls. Dot lifted her sunglasses and pointed to an empty spot for my axe and I fiddled with the unfamiliar fastenings as I tried to secure Bane. Eventually I managed it and settled into a seat with a blanket in the colour of sunsets – purples, oranges and pinks unnaturally bright in the dark interior.

"All ready?" Aloora twisted in her seat to give me a thumbs up. I strapped myself in and returned the gesture. With a grin, Aloora gave the horn a couple of toots as we set off, startling two students carrying heavy library books as we swerved into the road.

I watched the scenery change from terraced houses to more spaced out residential suburbs until we were finally on the main road out of Cardiff and towards the outskirts of the Breconian reserve. As we left the city behind, the road twined through green fields lined with ancient dry stone walls and the occasional dwelling. We climbed mountains at lazy inclines. The harsh bumping and rumbling as the van made its way along was far from restful. I stayed alert so I could direct Aloora towards Uncle Owain's wyrm farm. There was GPS in the van, but the postcode always led unsuspecting travellers to the middle of nowhere when they were trying to find the farm.

After a couple of hours of lurching along, and more fantasy music than I had even realised existed, we turned off on a winding track and the van bumped its way under a sign shaped like a dragon twisted around an anvil proclaiming: Haernson's Dragon Ranch.

I smiled at the small wyrms that raced us along the track as we approached, keeping pace with the van inside their enchanted metal enclosures and breathing small flames in their excitement. Errol scratched at the window, leaving claw marks on the glass as he matched their excitement with his own. I fought to keep him from breaking through the window as he tried to join the other wyrms.

Aloora pulled an unnecessary handbrake turn and we screeched to a halt outside a stone cottage surrounded by flameproof outbuildings.

I stared at my friend. She had only passed her test last year. She grinned over her shoulder, "I've gone on an advanced driving course for the Office. It was great! I've been waiting for a chance to use the skills in the real world!"

"Cool," I was surprised that my academic friend enjoyed dangerous driving, and partly wished she didn't as my stomach reeled from the sharp stop. I tumbled out, fighting to keep Errol in check and calling for my Uncle.

His husband, Dylan, came out from the ramshackle cottage holding a dishcloth. He enveloped me in a warm hug and mussed my hair up familiarly, "Good to see you Ame, Owain's out in the barn, preparing a stall for Errol," he greeted Aloora who had also stepped out, "I'll just put the kettle on, shall I?"

I thanked him and trotted over to the large red outbuilding. The large doors were open and I slowed as I entered, letting my eyes adjust to the gloom. "Ame!" boomed my uncle from an open stall. He strode over and gave me a bear hug. Errol squirmed his way free and began racing around in exhilarated circles.

Once I'd pulled free, I looked my uncle up and down. He looked as healthy as always with a ruddy complexion and a few fresh burns from the wyrms that called this place home.

I noticed his eyebrows had started to grow back since the last time I'd seen him, after a close call when trying out a new training method with a temperamental creature. His close cut beard on the other hand was a little charred.

My uncle wiped his hands on his leather apron and pulled out a lump of pure charcoal from his pocket. He held it out temptingly to Errol, who was still whizzing around us. "Sit," he commanded. Errol obeyed immediately. My uncle had a way with wyrms; that was why his farm was so successful. "Let's check out your home until your mistress gets back on her feet." He led Errol into the stall and my pet sniffed around before relieving himself in a corner, already thoroughly at home.

I opened my mouth to apologise but Uncle Owain waved me away, "It's natural, and it's good for the fire!" he laughed.

"Thanks for this O, it'll only be for a night or so,"

His eyes twinkled as he looked at me kindly and placed a large scarred hand on my shoulder, "Ame, sweetheart, your Dad told me what happened to your home, wyrms don't respond well to lots of change, it makes them nervous and prone to flames…and that gives those lunatics more chance to say these beautiful creatures are dangerous and get the law changed."

It had taken less time than I thought for him to get onto his pet topic of wyrm rights.

"So, I'll keep young Errol here until you're settled again. It's no bother, and he'll love it here." As if to emphasise his point, Errol had curled up and gone to sleep already. I decided not to fight right now and instead softly stroked my pet's head. I was going to miss him.

"Thanks. I'll pay you back," I choked a little as I said it, uncharacteristically emotional at handing over my Errol, even though he would be in good hands. It felt like I was betraying him, that I wasn't good enough to take care of him. Uncle Owain waved away my offer of payment. I tried again.

"If you insist, a bottle of Welsh whiskey will see me through the winter!" I smiled and pulled out my phone to write myself a note. As I pressed save, I saw my previous note to send through documents to the insurance company glaring at me accusingly. I swore, then had to explain myself to my Uncle.

He shook his head and tutted, obviously concerned, "You'd better get back to them quickly Ame, they like to drag their heels on these things as it is."

I nodded, "I know, I know. That's what the note is for. I'll do it as soon as I can." The thought briefly crossed my mind that we were heading into dragon territory and if they killed me, I wouldn't have to worry about insurance claims or what I was going to do in the meantime. I shook my head to clear such unproductive thoughts. I had to focus on the current job, not worry about the future unknowns. Once this mission was done, then I could worry about insurance documents.

As we walked across the yard to the van, I could see Dylan pressing a tin of something into Aloora's protesting hands. I looked at my Uncle, "That wouldn't be Dylan's famous fruit cake would it?"

Uncle Owain rubbed his hands together and gave me a wink, “Aye, it would. Just don’t let the driver have any. The amount of booze he put in there is enough to put me to sleep for a week!”

I laughed and gave him a hug as we got to the van.

“Are you sure you won’t stay for tea? I’ve got some welsh cakes just waiting to be eaten…” Dylan added temptingly. He was only happy if he was feeding someone. It was a good job that they both had an active life on the farm or they’d be heading for overweight instead of stocky.

I gave him a hug, “We’ll take some for the road, ta.” Dylan looked pleased and scurried back inside to fetch another tin and the small flat cakes.

Aloora gave me a grateful smile and retreated back into the driver’s seat to punch in the GPS coordinates for our rendez-vous with Agent Jones. I climbed into the van and saw Dot sleeping in the shady interior. She was so adept at living in the daylight that sometimes I forgot her natural cycle would have her wide awake at night time.

Dylan bustled back out and handed me an ancient tin that had come from some Christmas chocolates decades ago and gave me a scratchy kiss on the cheek. Owain pulled him back, “They want to get going!” and the two dwarves waved us off as we bumped down the muddy track back towards the main road.

I felt guilty about abandoning my pet but also relieved that he had somewhere to stay and I trusted Owain to look after him well. It might also mean that Aloora’s housemates would be more inclined to let me stay for a bit longer, I knew they weren't fans of the wyrm, and pets were probably not included in their rental contracts.

As we drove, the rich green fields passed in a blur as Aloora made full use of her advanced driving skills and took us swiftly around sharp corners. White dots indicated fluffy sheep grazing in the rain, while the grey smudges were rundown abandoned stone buildings. The Welsh mountain roads weren't made for this type of driving and I was flung across my seat. I gripped the webbing nearest me for support as we swerved our way towards the Breconia reserve. Dot managed to sleep through it all, her head bobbing each time Aloora made a turn.

We made it in one piece to a track where Agent Jones was waiting for us, wearing a mountain jacket that perfectly complimented her copper skin and jeans. She still looked put together, but I had never seen her so dressed down. I had been expecting her to be wearing one of her trouser suits with a sharply pressed jacket.

She motioned to Aloora to move along and climbed into the driving seat herself, immediately turning off the radio. "Right, the situation hasn't changed. If anything the dragons are getting more agitated. We're going to be working with the elves on this one. Stay sharp."

With that cryptic message, she set off, easing the van into gear. Her driving was sedate compared to Aloora's and I leaned back in my seat, watching the rain trickle down the window. My stomach had lurched at the mention of elves and I wondered if a certain blonde elf with green eyes would turn up.

Chapter 10

As we got closer to the reserve, I noticed a white vapour form across the fields, swallowing up the verdant green with snaking tendrils of fog. The mist crept over the fields towards the road and thickened until we were driving through a cloud. Agent Jones gripped the steering wheel tightly and kept going, her amber eyes squinting at the fog.

Condensation formed on the windows as the temperature dropped. I reached inside my backpack for my enchanting goggles and pulled them over my eyes. I could now see any magical auras. Dot was a dull red and my friend's gnomish aura glowed violet under the specially tinted lenses. I stared at Agent Jones. I knew she was a shifter, but no aura showed up thanks to her magic dampening bracelet, it really was very effective.

We had slowed to a crawl and the mist was thickening. I could no longer see the end of the van's stumpy bonnet. I looked out of the window and drew in a breath. Through my goggles, I could clearly see the pink outline of fae auras in the terrifying shape of ten-legged tarfangtulas. Schiztz.

There was a pack of them moving towards the van, slowly, taking their time. Their legs looked no less horrible for moving slowly or being outlined in a soft, swirling, baby pink colour thanks to my goggles.

"Tarfangtulas incoming!" I whispered to the others, as if keeping my voice down would prevent them sensing us.

Aloora nodded thoughtfully, "Tarfangtulas are kept within the boundaries of the Breconian woods; they can't leave the reserve thanks to the wards the elves have put up."

I didn't want facts.

"Er, we're trying to go *into* the Breconian woods!" I pointed out, eyeing the creatures, which were now getting even closer. I imagined I could see ten bulbous eyes seeking us out. Agent Jones was still edging the van forwards, creeping along the now invisible road.

I unbuckled my seatbelt and stood. I was short, but still managed to bump my head on the roof of the van. "Schiztz!" I swore and rubbed my head as I crouched and stumbled over to where Bane was strapped to the wall of the van. I fumbled with the fastenings as I worked to undo it. When the tarfangtulas got here, I wanted to be holding a weapon.

Dot groaned and rubbed her forehead, "What's happening?" she grumbled sleepily.

"Tarfangtulas!" I hissed. No one else seemed worried about them.

"I hate those things!" At least Dot was on my side. She pulled the sword I had enchanted for the Magical Liaison

Office from where it was fastened securely to the wall of the van. I envied her smoothness as I worked to free Bane.

Aloora turned to me, "They shouldn't attack unless provoked, we just need to get past the ward and out of this mist…"

It was at that point that one of the creatures leapt and landed on the roof of the van. We all jumped at the impact as the roof dented with the imprint of its large, clawed legs. I looked up instinctively and saw its hideous form bathed in a pink glow.

"You were saying…"

Aloora paled and looked upwards in time to see another tarfangtula loom out of the mist and step onto the bonnet of the vehicle. It brought its ugly head to the windscreen and shrieked, opening its mouth wide and showing its teeth behind its mouth parts.

She screamed. Agent Jones had pulled a crossbow from somewhere and was aiming it at the creature. "Dragonquest!" she barked my friend's last name, "Remember your training! Get a weapon!"

Aloora nodded and clambered over the front seats to the back of the van where Dot and I were crouching low. She grabbed herself a crossbow and, trembling, pointed it upwards.

More of the large spiders were crowding around the van now, and we were jostled from side to side as they fought to get in. Agent Jones was still managing to edge us forwards one-handed as she aimed at the creature fighting to get in the windshield.

“Can it smash the glass?” I asked the relevant question.

Dot stuck her tongue out as she considered, “We had the glass toughened since our last outing in Dan so it should hold…”

“Dan?”

“Dan the van,” she looked at me as if that was obvious.

The creatures were climbing all over the van, their sharp claws scrabbling for purchase.

“Dzrak this!” exclaimed Agent Jones and she accelerated hard into the fog, running over one of the arachnids with a large bump. She swerved from left to right, shaking others off the roof. I fell to the floor hard, facing upwards. It was satisfying to hear the crunch as they hit the tarmac and I enjoyed seeing their pink auras fly off the vehicle.

They kept coming. More of the creatures raced after us. We were surrounded. I pushed myself up then stopped, staring at the charred imprint of the fire rune on the floor of the van. With a word, I had activated the rune and the van blazed into flames. The tarfangtulas on the roof gave a piercing shriek and leapt off in pain. The others backed off, staying a respectful distance away from the flames.

Agent Jones turned in her seat and nodded to me to keep it up before rolling down the window and shooting a crossbow bolt out. A scream of pain told us she’d hit her mark and I wondered how she could tell where to aim.

I placed my hand on the rune, willing my magic to bolster the enchantment and the flames burned more intensely, pushing the creatures back. Belatedly, I tried to put a barrier between the flames and the engine to avoid an explosion.

The fire gave the mist a strange orangey glow, but it didn't lift. I looked around, we were still surrounded by spiders. Then, behind the pink tarfangtula auras, I saw a band of forest green humanoid shapes. Elves.

"Stop shooting!" I screamed at the shifter over the sound of the blazing inferno that was engulfing the van as my magic intensified the fire. Agent Jones raised her eyebrow at me, unused to taking orders. "Elves!" I explained, pointing to the right, before turning my attention back to the rune.

She muttered something and slowed down, keeping us moving forward. The elves moved fast and their green auras zipped around, ducking and weaving between the giant spiders. The pink auras faded as they died and the remaining tarfangtulas, sensing they were losing, retreated quickly, scurrying away on their ten long legs.

The elves surrounded the van and walked beside us as we crept through the mist. Eventually, the haze began to thin out and disappeared as quickly as it had arrived. Agent Jones stopped the vehicle and I heard a voice shout, "Put the fire out!" and looked guiltily down at the rune I was still activating.

I removed my hand and deactivated it. Agent Jones rolled her eyes at me, "Good job I had Maxi take a look at the engine. It's a lot less flammable this time."

Before I could ask what she meant, an elf appeared right by her window while she was twisting to look at me. She turned back and jumped a little as she saw the attractive golden face at her open window. I smirked to see her unprepared for something, but she recovered quickly.

“What was that?” she barked, “Why are the tarfangtulas so close to your borders?”

The handsome elf blinked in the face of direct questioning and then narrowed his eyes, unused to be spoken to like that, “I will ask the questions. Who are you and what are you doing in the realm of Breconia?”

After a bit of posturing from both of them, Agent Jones convinced the elf we had an appointment with the Captain of the guards and he should escort us to the city. The elf pulled out a walkie talkie, which looked at odds with his elegant grey and gold uniform and instead informed us that he would take us to the car park because vehicles were not permitted past a certain point in the reserve.

Chapter 11

Agent Jones parked the van sedately in the gravel car park, the tyres crunching on the loose stones. I got out, still nursing my bruised head and looked around. It was the first time I'd been to the Breconian reserve. It was beautiful. The mist still hung in a light barrier around the borders but in the reserve, the sun was shining and it appeared golden. A marked difference to the grey rain we had just been driving in.

The edge of the carpark fell away steeply into a lush, green valley. I heard the gushing of water and followed the turquoise river that meandered lazily along the valley floor until I found the steep waterfall. It cascaded down past a rocky outcrop, splashing droplets creating a bright rainbow as it fell into a large pool before flowing onwards through the vale. A small herd of deer were drinking from it peacefully.

Beyond the vale were large mountains and a wild forest, with trees almost as tall as the apartment blocks in the city. Something moved in the shadows and I reminded myself that, for all its beauty, Breconia was home to many wild creatures; including tarfangtulas. I pulled myself away from the scenery as my head began to swim at the height. I joined Agent Jones who was listening to a tall elf with shoulder-length blond hair and a firm expression. Unlike his companions, his uniform was green rather than grey, trimmed with gold. I had a charm that made me immune to elven glamour, but the annoying truth was, they were always attractive. I was glad that Agent Jones seemed to be ignoring the pull of their charm.

"…other side of the mountain. The dragons seem to be more restless at sunset, so you'll get a chance to see their erratic behaviour for yourselves. They've been roaming further and further, but they always seem to come back."

I put my hand up. Agent Jones rolled her eyes at me and motioned for me to speak, "Er, why doesn't the barrier stop the dragons, like the giant spiders?"

Aloora replied before the authoritative elf could, "Dragons are highly magical creatures, very difficult to overpower or contain, as you've seen. The particular ward around Breconia is highly effective at both containment and keeping unwelcome visitors out, but it can't match the dragons' power."

"Now the lesson is over," the guard glowered at me, "perhaps we can make a move?" He was impatient to get going, but Agent Jones made him wait while she checked over our kit. She gave me a grunt of approval as I fitted Bane into a leather loop on a belt that I had borrowed from the Office.

In a fit of inspiration, I retrieved the battered tin from the van and handed out Welsh cakes. Pointedly, none of the elven guards took them. I shrugged and munched my way through three of the small, sweet disks of goodness before we left. I shoved the rest into my backpack and one into my pocket for later.

I tried to judge the distance to the mountain and failed miserably. It took us over an hour to descend into the valley, picking our way down uneven roots that the elves used as steps. They were spread out to accommodate an elven pace and it was uncomfortable going for my shorter legs. I kept my eyes firmly on the knotted wooden roots, not trusting my vertigo to cope with both amazing views and keeping my balance.

We finally made it to the thick grass on the valley floor. I wheezed some air back into my lungs whilst the others discussed the route.

"It's not long until sunset," I whispered to Dot.

She was reapplying factor fifty sun cream to the small pockets of skin visible beneath a peaked hat and sunglasses, "Less than an hour," she agreed.

I looked across the river, which was a lot wider than it had looked from the top of the cliff. The mountains lay beyond it and the dragons were the other side of the peak. How were we going to get there? I chewed my lip as I tried to puzzle it out.

While I was looking at the distance to cross, I heard a gasp and quickly turned my attention back to the group. Aloora was looking upwards at the clear blue sky. I followed her gaze and made out several dots getting closer. I rested my hand on my axe, ready for the threat from above. No one else seemed worried and I frowned as the creatures came into view.

Golden bodies glinted in the sunlight as they swooped down towards us. Gryphons. Their lion paws landed lightly on the grass and they folded their large golden wings against their backs neatly. Their riders dismounted with an easy jump. These elves wore the same grey and gold uniform as the elves who had escorted us this far, but had metal helmets strapped onto their heads.

They saluted the elf in green armour and lined up precisely. I ignored them and stared at the creatures who were regally ignoring us. Their curved beaks were a burnished gold colour, almost rose gold, and their eyes were a sparkling blue. One of them met my gaze fiercely and cawed. I looked away, forcing my attention to the others.

To my horror, they were starting to mount the winged beasts, each member of the Magical Liaison Office accompanied by an elf.

"Oh, no, no no no! I can't ride that!" I was suddenly alarmed at the prospect of flying to our destination, "I'll walk, I'll meet you there."

Agent Jones gave me a critical look, "It would take far too long to walk, but if you insist, you can camp overnight on the mountain and we'll see you in the morning."

I gulped. A night in the open here, where tarfangtulas and who knows what else lurked unseen. I clenched and unclenched my fists and willed my mind to think of another option.

Aloora grinned down at me, "Come on, it'll be fun!"

"You're just obsessed with flying creatures," I complained. I walked reluctantly to a gryphon and swallowed hard.

An elf climbed astride in one easy motion and looked down at me with scorn on her face as she offered me a hand. The gryphon turned its majestic head towards me and then bent its neck. It nuzzled at my pocket. I retrieved the Welsh cake I had stashed there for later and held it out, my palm flat. It pecked it like a duck and gobbled it up. It clicked its tongue at me and gave a chirp. Tentatively, I placed my hand on its soft feathers.

"Please, don't kill me OK?" I pleaded softly. I wanted to be proud but I knew I needed help to get up so I took the elf's proffered hand and clambered on, adjusting my axe and backpack as best I could. There was no saddle and its back was comfortable.

"Ready?" asked the elf as she flicked the leather reins attached to a harness around the creature's head. Before I had a chance to answer, the gryphon had stretched out its huge golden wings and leapt upwards. I jolted forwards and screamed as I gripped its neck tightly. It shook its head a couple of times and shrieked in shock before recovering. I bit my lip to stop me crying out again and peeked down at the shrinking ground. Big mistake. I felt my stomach heave as we climbed higher into the sky. I closed my eyes in an effort to stop the dizziness and forced myself to breathe slowly. I heard the elf mutter something behind my back. From the tone, I guessed it was something like: "Bloody dwarves."

It felt like we were in the sky for an eternity and the rushing air had numbed my fingers and toes as we flew across the valley towards the mountain. We landed softly and I tumbled from the gryphon, thankful to have my feet back on solid ground.

Agent Jones gave me an amused look and carried on talking to the elves. It sounded like we were splitting up into teams and trying to get closer to the dragons.

No one checked I was alright and I forced myself to my feet. As I looked around, I realised we were still the wrong side of the mountain. “Why didn’t the gryphons drop us off any closer?” I complained quietly.

Aloora was close enough to hear me, “We don’t want to aggravate the dragons, just get near enough to figure out what’s wrong.”

Well, that told me. A couple of the elves were giving me sideways glances, so I readjusted my axe pointedly and squared my shoulders.

“Right,” Agent Jones barked, “Amethyst, you’re with Dot. Aloora, you’re with me. Let’s go.”

“Can’t I be with Aloora?” I asked hopefully.

She shook her head, “Aloora is the only one who’s got a hope of understanding Draconic, she’s with me.”

She set off at a brisk pace, easily keeping up with two elves who had tagged along. I fell into step behind them, panting as I tried to keep up. The remaining elves stayed with the gryphons, trying to keep the beasts calm as they scented the larger predators just over the crest of the mountain.

We crossed the peak quickly, picking our way over rocky outcrops. I tried not to look down as the single path narrowed further and then disappeared into a grey ledge overlooking a sheer drop. Agent Jones halted and pulled some rope from her pack. Deftly she knotted us all together before we crossed the ledge. The surefooted elves declined to be strapped to us and walked along the tiny shelf easily. They sat on the edge of a large rock on the other side, swinging their legs into the air and looking thoroughly at home. Bloody elves.

The rocky shelf jutted out about three feet and the others walked cautiously but quickly. I was terrified and edged my way along, my face pressed into the stone as if I could draw strength from the mountain itself. The rope soon grew taught and I realised I was holding the others back. I tried to speed up but my feet felt like lead in my sturdy boots.

Dot noticed my discomfort and offered to hold my hand in case I fell. The offer was kindly meant, but the thought of falling made me more afraid and I clung to the face of the mountain and inched my way along.

"Come on!" I heard Agent Jones bellow impatiently. "It'll be dark soon!"

The thought of being stuck high up on this outcrop in the dark filled me with more fear and I forced my legs to move.

"That's it. One step at a time. Easy does it. Nearly there," Dot was more sympathetic than her boss.

I risked turning my face and realised we were almost to the end. Agent Jones and Aloora were already on the large rock with the elves and getting ready to unbuckle themselves from the strong climbing rope.

I sighed in relief and took a large step. My foot slipped on the sheer rock and I panicked. My arms cartwheeled wildly as I tried frantically to regain my balance. Then I was falling. An image of my broken body, lying at the foot of the mountain filled my head and I opened my mouth to scream. A cold hand grasped my wrist tightly and I froze in shock. My wild eyes found Dot's calm face.

"It's OK, I've got you," she smiled, showing her fangs. She pulled me easily back up to the ledge and shifted her grip to my clammy hand. She took the other one as I hyperventilated and looked deep into my eyes. "It will be alright, we're just walking."

I felt soothed. I trusted her and her stillness and confidence was almost tangible. Then she calmly walked backwards, facing me and keeping eye contact as she led me to where the others were waiting. With a toothy grin, she undid the ropes binding us together and set off after Agent Jones, who had no time for near death experiences. I felt the fog of calm that had stilled my mind lift. Had I really nearly fallen off the side of a mountain?

Aloora flung herself at me and squeezed hard. I hugged her back, trembling slightly as reality hit me, and we held hands on the wider path until it was time to part. When Agent Jones gave the order to split up, I almost refused to let her go. My friend gave me a final hug and went to stand next to Agent Jones and one of the elves. Dot met my eyes and gave me a thumbs up. It looked like everyone else was ready.

I had a choice, I supposed; I could refuse to go where I was told and be sent back across the death ledge alone or I could stay with Dot and spy on some dragons. I'd survived dragons before. I chose to follow Dot.

As we started to move off with the Captain of the guards in tow, Aloora shouted out, "Wait!" She ran over to our group holding a large tub of hand cream. She opened it and a tangy sulphurous aroma hit my nostrils.

"What the dzrak is that, Ally?" I coughed.

She scooped some greenish cream out and smeared it on my face before I had a chance to back away. I gagged at the smell.

"It will hide your scent from the dragons," she beamed, "I had it made specially."

She held the pot out to the elf and vampire. The elf turned green and took a small amount with the end of his fingers. He couldn't bring himself to rub it on his face and instead daubed it onto his clothes. Dot curled her lip and forced herself to take some of the cream and rub it on her skin.

Suitably stinkified, we set off again. This side of the mountain was grassier than the other and the incline less steep and treacherous. I lifted my gaze from my feet and took in the view as we descended. There were high peaks surrounding us, all covered with stubby green grass. Large rocks jutted out of the ground, worn smooth from centuries of exposure to the elements. The setting sun gave the scenery a golden glow as if magic had settled visibly on the land.

A mountain goat with curling horns leapt in fright as we passed and raced off. It gambolled away over the short grass and disappeared behind a ruined stone hut.

“Who’d choose to live up here?” I remarked, breaking the silence in our group.

The elf deigned to reply, “It’s a ty unnos. There’s a lot of them round here, mostly abandoned now.”

I looked at Dot; her face was as puzzled as mine. “What’s a tee eenos?” I mangled the pronunciation.

“It’s translates as ‘one-night house’. There was an old law that if you could build a house in one night and have a fire burning in the hearth then you could keep the land it was on. Up here, it was easy enough to grab stones and grasses to build the dwelling but harder to live. No one lives up here now.”

“You’re all slumming it in Breconia,” I joked. The elven city was said to be splendid and about as far from a slum as you could get. The Captain didn’t laugh.

I rolled my eyes behind his back and we entered a wood on the side of the mountain. The trees were spindly and tall. Their leaves had begun to turn from green to yellow. The setting sun leant them a golden shimmer. The elf forged ahead as the light faded. I kept my eyes on the ground to avoid tripping on any tree roots, so I didn’t notice when he stopped. I walked straight into his back, gaining a glare from the Captain and a smirk from Dot.

He hissed at me to “Shhhh!” then lay on his stomach and inched forward over the springy moss. I copied him, using my elbows to drag myself forward slowly. He stopped and I pulled myself alongside and forced myself not to swear. The mossy floor gave way suddenly to a pit. I studied the cut slate sides and guessed it was a disused quarry.

A roar broke into my musings and I snapped my head up. A huge white dragon descended into the pit. The female. Its wings created a strong gust of wind and I lowered my head against the force of it. It landed softly. The fading light gave it an ethereal glow. The red dragon joined it with a rumbling growl. Slate shingles fell from the sides of the pit. Fire spurted from its nostrils and it paced the pit angrily. It clawed at the larger rocks jutting out and tipped them over with ease. It seemed smaller than I remembered when I'd first encountered it. Maybe it was because it was next to the massive female. Or maybe it was because I was seeing it unconfined by the cellar underneath Cardiff Castle. I shuddered at the terrifying memory and forced my attention back to the present.

I looked up, waiting for the third dragon, the adolescent. It swooped above us, appearing over the quarry only to fly away again. At an exasperated growl from the white female, the smaller dragon flew directly upright then descended in a dive at a frightening speed. I braced myself for a crash. Just before it hit the ground, it pulled up. Its wings created dust clouds as it landed.

The red dragon bit the younger one sharply on its neck. The teenager gave a shriek of pain then growled and curled up in a sulky sleeping pose. I had no idea dragons had family dynamics. The red beast settled too, curling its tail round its body in a pose that reminded me painfully of my pet wyrm. I hoped he was alright at Uncle Owain's farm.

The female did a circuit of the quarry, her head low. As she passed under our hiding spot, her nostrils flared and she looked up. I held my breath. This was it. She knew we were here. She narrowed her eyes and then sneezed. A blast of ice shot into the far wall, causing a minor avalanche of slate to fall loudly onto the floor. She shook her huge head, twisting her sinewy neck. A strange crooning sound came from her. I thought it almost sounded sad. The red male lifted his head and gave an answering call. The female joined her family and they settled down.

We watched them sleep until it got dark. I pulled my enchanting goggles on and stared. The golden auras surrounding the dragons was immense. I had to squint through the tinted brown lenses to avoid being blinded. I felt a hand on my shoulder and twisted sharply. Dot's dull red aura swirled into view. She tilted her head towards the woods. We were going. I nodded, instinctively keeping silent. The vampire disappeared into the trees. I could see her crawling next to the elf's forest green aura. I took one look back at the dragons.

As I began to edge myself backwards, I felt the ground shift beneath me. The side of the quarry was collapsing! I tried to push myself up and run onto solid ground, but the landslide had started. I was dragged down to the floor of the pit in a cacophony of falling slate. I felt my body twist as the stones pulled me with them. The sharp slates cut into my skin. I bit my lip to keep myself from crying out. Dust cloaked my throat.

I felt the rocks settle on top of me. I tentatively moved an arm. Slates shifted noisily, but I could move. I held my breath as I forced myself to sit. My head swam as I tried to orientate myself. The main avalanche had happened next to me and a large pile of fresh rubble was heaped to my left.

Anxiously, I looked around the quarry. The dragons' auras were blinding through my goggles. As I tried to focus, I realised that three enormous heads were facing in my direction.

Chapter 12

I froze. My eyes darted around, looking for a way out. The steep sides would be a challenge even for an experienced climber. I could make out Dot and the Captain's auras as they crouched cautiously at the edge of the pit. Dot was gesturing frantically. I thought I could make out the auras of the other team too, glowing faintly further back. At least there would be witnesses to my demise.

The teenage dragon rose and prowled towards me. Schiztz. It bent its head and sniffed. I held my breath. My hand inched its way slowly to the comforting weight of my axe, still attached to my belt and buried beneath a thin layer of slate. The dragon clawed at the rubble. It shifted its head from side to side. I allowed myself a brief moment of hope. Maybe the disgusting cream had worked and it couldn't smell me. Maybe it would give up and go back to sleep.

As it seemed to lose interest, the sound of more slate shifting came from above. Another avalanche! I turned my head involuntarily. The noise was coming from directly above me. The dragon had turned towards the sound too and missed my movement. It started to beat its wings to avoid the new rock fall. I was certain that I would be buried alive. I pushed myself upwards, ignoring my complaining muscles and began to run.

The shingles shifted beneath my feet. I slipped and surfed to the side of the quarry. I looked over my shoulder into the angry eyes of the dragon. My feet caught on a rock and I fell forwards. I hit the rubble hard. Before I could recover, I felt myself tugged backwards. I braced myself for pain.

Surprisingly, it didn't come. No claws were tearing into my skin. Instead, I felt myself leave the ground. The dragon was taking off and taking me with it. Schiztz. I frantically twisted to try to hit at the hard claws with my hands. To no avail. It ignored me as if I was an ant. It flew higher and higher. I watched as the magical auras of my teammates shrunk.

I tried to think through my panic. It was gripping my backpack rather than me. I had to act before it got too high. I forced myself to shake one arm free of its strap. It was harder than it sounded in my head, and I nearly dislocated my arm as it slipped free. I shifted and clung onto the bag. I panted and then freed my other arm. Wind blew my hair around my face. I heard a tear as the strap I was dangling from began to rip. I angled myself so my feet were facing the ground. I began a countdown in my head. Three…Two… The strap broke. I plunged towards the ground.

I looked up at the golden aura. It was strangely beautiful, I thought as I plummeted to my end. The creature didn't seem to notice I had fallen and carried on with its prize. I hoped it liked Welsh cakes and baggy t-shirts or it would be sorely disappointed.

I hit the top of a tree hard. I wanted to cry out, but the next branch winded me. I managed to grab onto it for a brief second before it gave way. I flailed wildly. Despite colliding with every branch on the way down, I didn't manage to grab another one and I hit the ground hard. I tried to swear, but the breath had left my body. I lay there, gasping and in pain. I looked up at the glimpses of stars I could see through the hole I had made in the wooded canopy. They were beautiful. One large red star loomed larger over me. I frowned. The star had Dot's voice.

"Thank goodness you were bleeding or it would have taken forever to find you!"

I blinked. A snarky reply formed in my head, but my mouth wouldn't cooperate in forming the words. I ended up saying, "Wha-"

The star that may have been Dot, was now rubbing something onto my body. It smelled of mint, aniseed and whisky. I winced as a burning sensation coursed through me, followed by a cooling relief. As I came to my senses, I recognised the effects of *Madam Mim's Cure All*. A potent healing potion that magical beings swore by.

"Thank goodness that dragon carried you off, I wasn't sure we'd be able to get you out of the quarry until morning if it hadn't!" Dot continued as she checked me over.

My mouth fell open. I didn't even have a reply to that. It hadn't felt lucky to be carried off by a creature the size of a bus.

"We'd better move. All the dragons took flight after the rock slide. It's best if we get back to the gryphons and make it to Breconia as soon as we can. Nothing seems to be badly broken, can you stand?" Without waiting for a reply, Dot grabbed my arm and heaved me upright. Pain coursed through me, but it was dulled by the *Cure All*. She hoisted me over her slim shoulder in a fireman's lift and began to run. Her chunky knit jumper was soft as I jolted along, dazed and feeling sick as she raced with vampire speed through the forest. I tried to lift my head at one point and got hit by a low hanging branch for my trouble.

My night vision is pretty good thanks to my dwarven heritage, but Dot's was another level. She weaved between the tightly packed trees with ease and we reached the edge of the wood in record time. She put me down gently as she surveyed the surroundings, seeking out the best route back.

"Where are the others?" I croaked. My mouth was still dry from the dust I'd swallowed in the landslide.

"They're making their own way back. It's safer if we're not all together, the dragons won't be able to pick us off so easily," she spoke dispassionately.

"Can I have a drink?" I gasped.

She shook her head, "Sorry, the only drink I'm carrying is one you won't want." I tried to will some saliva into my mouth. It was tempting to disagree with her, but I wasn't desperate enough to drink blood…yet.

I swept my gaze over the open landscape. My goggles picked out a faint greenish glow. I squinted. That was elven magic. I pointed, "What's over there?"

Dot looked in the direction of my finger, “It’s the old ruined house we saw, why?”

“Can we hide there? It looks like there’s an enchantment on it.”

Dot looked from me to the stone house, “I don’t know…we should try to reach the gryphons,” she looked me up and down. A throaty roar interrupted us. My heart plummeted. “On the other hand, a place to hide sounds great!”

She picked me up again and I clung on as she raced across the grass to the hut. As we slipped inside, I felt the sensation of leafy forests. An elven spell. I looked around. The small house appeared to be run down, missing part of its roof. There was something else though that I couldn’t place. Dot paced the small room, glancing up every so often as she listened for signs the dragons were coming.

I pulled my keyring from my pocket and rubbed the charm Gunther had given me to ward against elven glamour. I didn’t know if it worked against other types of elf magic but it made me feel better to be doing something. I closed my eyes and focused. There was another spell, still elven, but with a slightly different feel to it in the corner farthest from the door. Curious, I crawled over to the corner. Dirt and old straw were piled up over the earthen floor. I kicked the dried mud aside with my boot. Something clinked. I frowned, puzzled and kicked out again. There was definitely something there.

“What the…?” I muttered as I scuffed the straw away, trying to find whatever was there.

Dot stopped pacing and joined me, “What are you doing?”

"There's something here."

She stood over me as I scrabbled around. My hands connected with something cool and metallic. A large iron ring. I risked getting out my phone. It had a crack across the screen from its recent adventures in my pocket as I had fallen into a quarry and then from a dragon's claws. Miraculously, it still worked and I flicked on the torch setting. I pointed it at the floor and saw that there was an iron ring, looking suspiciously new on an old wooden trapdoor.

I met Dot's gaze. We were both intrigued. I began to pull it, but couldn't shift the door. Dot stepped forward and, with one hand, wrenched it up. As I shone the torch into it, I froze. There, nestled into a small gap dug into the floor was a jewelled dragon's egg. Its ruby exterior reflected my torchlight. Strangely, it didn't have a golden draconic aura under the gaze of my enchanting goggles, but rather a forest green, elven one. A concealment charm perhaps? I didn't know enough about elven magic to guess.

I lifted my goggles and turned to ask Dot if she thought this was why the dragons were acting erratically. She was already pulling out her own phone to call in the find to Agent Jones. As she was dialling, she stopped and looked at the door. She waved for me to turn off my torch. I fumbled with the buttons but couldn't turn it off. I shoved it under my top, just as the unsteady door creaked open. An elf entered. The Captain. He saw me immediately with his superior night vision. Dot was out of his eye line and the shadows around her seemed to have darkened.

"What are you doing here?" he demanded.

"Hiding from the dragon," I replied, "what are you doing here?"

He paused, "Looking for you. Thank goodness you're alright. Come on, I'll get you back to the others." His voice was smooth and, if it wasn't for the hesitation, I would have bought the act.

"You're not checking on the egg then?" I chanced it.

"How did…What are you talking about?" He clearly wasn't going to win any poker tournaments, "I think you'd better come with me."

I stayed put. He took one step towards me, his hand at the sharp sword by his side. I grabbed my phone from under my top and aimed the torchlight into his eyes. He stopped and blinked as the harsh light ruined his vision.

Dot exploded from the dark corner in a blur of speed. She pushed the elf against the wall, hard. I heard the crack of his golden helmet against the stone wall. He struggled to pull his sword free. She caught the motion and grabbed his hand hard. I heard a crunch of bone. The elf paled. He tried to pull away. She was too strong. Her hand closed around his neck and she squeezed. A strange gurgling came from his throat. He clawed at her slender fingers then went limp. Her hand stayed at his neck.

"Dot," I called, then more urgently, "Dot!"

She turned to me, her eyes glowing red. She bared her fangs.

"Dot!"

She shook her head and her face transformed back to its usual cheerful self. She removed her hand from the

Captain's neck and he crumpled to the floor. The torchlight was swaying wildly as my hands trembled. Dot took out her own phone and called Agent Jones.

We were instructed to stay put until morning as the dragons were still roaming the skies. I was exhausted but too much adrenaline coursed through me for comfortable sleep. I managed to drop off eventually while Dot kept watch over the Captain.

A rap on the door woke me, earlier than I would have liked. I got up painfully from the floor. As well as the bruises and cuts from yesterday, I had a crick in my neck from sleeping on the ground. Agent Jones entered immediately with a curt nod to me and Dot. She chucked me a water bottle. I fumbled the catch and it fell to the ground. I picked it up unceremoniously and took a long swig, grateful for the sweet water. As I was gulping down the liquid, a tall elf in an elegant, richly embroidered tunic entered the shack with another elf I recognised. Lorandir.

I was so shocked, I choked on the water. He was by my side in an instant and I felt his healing magic engulf me. I relaxed into the familiar feel of honeyed mead, bitter chocolate and mossy forests. I felt my body recover properly, in a way that the *Cure All* could never achieve. The other elf coughed pointedly and Lorandir retreated to his side, leaving me to get my breath back.

"Where is it?" he commanded.

I bristled, "What's the magic word?"

I saw Lorandir hastily turn a snort of laughter into a cough. The elf ignored me and turned to Agent Jones,

"There was talk of a dragon egg. Did you call me so I could be insulted?"

Agent Jones pinched the bridge of her nose. It had clearly been a long night for her as well, "Just get the egg for King Lireath, Amethyst."

My eyes bulged. Oops. Sarcasm with royalty didn't go down well. I quickly bent to retrieve the ruby coloured egg from the dirty hatch. Reverently, I lifted it. It was warm to the touch, and slightly rough as if it were a large geode formed from crystals. I still couldn't feel any draconic magic emanating from it. In the beams of sunlight streaming through the damaged roof, it seemed to glow. I held it close to my chest and turned. The King's hands were already outstretched, reaching for it. His eyes were full of greed. I hesitated for one moment, unwilling to hand over the beautiful egg.

"Come on Haernson," Agent Jones snapped at me.

I placed the egg gently into the King's long slender hands. He smiled brightly.

"I will ensure this is returned to the dragons," he was interrupted by a moan at knee height behind him. He turned and gave the Captain a withering look. "It my deepest regret that my own Captain was found to be behind this theft. I will ensure he is dealt with severely."

Agent Jones stepped forward, "I need to take him to the Office for questioning before we decide if we can hand him over to your custody."

"What?!" The King was unused to having his authority questioned.

Agent Jones shrugged, "It's standard protocol, and I believe it was you who signed your people up to the Magical Accord when the Office was formed…"

The King narrowed his eyes at our leader and seemed about to argue. He clearly thought better of it and a bright smile crossed his face, changing his bitter expression completely, "Of course, where would we be without the Accord? You will be in touch." It was a statement.

Agent Jones gave a tiny nod and he swept out. Lorandir gave me a quick wink and followed in his wake. Dot and Agent Jones tied up the Captain with climbing rope and led him out. Tiredness swept over me suddenly. I forced my feet to walk and I trudged behind them.

Outside, I saw Aloora giving the elven King a lecture and handing over her disgusting sulphurous cream. I smiled; typical Aloora behaviour. She saw me and bounded over, cutting her lecture short.

"Thank goodness you're alright Ame! How do you always get into these situations?!" She wrapped her arms around me. I stared at her head as I returned the embrace. I hadn't exactly planned to fall into a quarry or be airlifted by a monstrous creature.

"Don't even worry about it," I forced a smile. My stomach rumbled loudly, breaking up our reunion. "Got any food?"

She shook her head and retrieved a healthy grain bar from her backpack. I thought longingly of the tin of Welsh cakes in my own bag, now in the custody of a dragon. I was hungry though so forced myself to eat the snack.

“What now?” I asked between bites.

“Back to Cardiff. The elves are handling returning the egg to the dragon. Did you see it? It must be the first dragon egg laid in over four thousand years! The theft was clearly why they were acting so strangely. I got some great recordings! I’ll have to go over them with Professor Maron as soon as we get back! I can’t wait!” she finally took a breath.

“I don’t suppose there’s another, easier route back?” I couldn’t keep the hope from my voice.

Aloora nodded, “The dragons have already left their nest. We saw them swoop West, probably still looking for their egg,” a touch of sadness entered her voice, “that Captain did a good job with magically concealing it from them. I told the King that will need to be reversed before they attempt to replace it…”

I stared at her and interrupted quickly before I got a sermon on dragon eggs, “And that means what for us?”

She blinked and smiled broadly. My friend gestured behind me, “It means the gryphons can take us all the way back to the van!”

I groaned loudly.

Chapter 13

I was glad I'd only had a small cereal bar as I nearly threw up after the gryphon flight. Agent Jones insisted on driving back to Cardiff. I was thankful for her steadier approach to driving. I didn't think I could stand Aloora's hair-raising techniques today. Dot and I stayed vigilant as we drove back through the mist that represented the warded edges of the elven territory. I peered anxiously through my enchanting goggles, tapping the studded leather straps nervously as we passed through.

No pink spider-like auras appeared. We made it through and back onto the comforting tarmac of the mundane Welsh roads. Dot closed her eyes the instant we were through. It was so easy to forget she was nocturnal. About ten minutes from the Breconian border, I dozed off as well.

I was awoken rudely by my phone as we were still driving through the lush Welsh countryside. The sun was low but bright in the pale blue sky. I answered without checking the caller I.D.

"Where are you?"

I groaned as I recognised the musical female voice, angry at me. I hadn't called her to cancel our session today.

"Sorry Es, I got caught up."

"It's Espretha not Es. And what is more important than a training session?"

"Well, I got caught up in Breconia…"

"Breconia?" she interrupted quietly, "What were you doing there?"

I hadn't had any time to think anything up, so I answered honestly, "Helping with a dragon problem."

"I see," she inhaled sharply, "and I suppose Lorandir was there."

I nodded then remembered she couldn't see me, "Well yes, but I didn't really get a chance to speak to him. He was healing me then…"

"Of course he was. He always loves to play the knight in shining armour, regardless of whether you want rescuing" she sounded bitter.

"I'll be in Cardiff later today, we can train this afternoon," I offered, trying to change the topic.

"What makes you think I don't have things to do?" she replied sharply. I winced at her tone.

"Sorry, of course you do. Rain check?"

"It's forecast to be bright and sunny all day," I heard the confusion in her voice. Sometimes elven culture was a completely different world.

"OK, so when do you want to train next?"

"This afternoon is fine. Three p.m. Don't be late." She hung up. I groaned again, knowing she was going to spend the time until then thinking up a torturous warm up routine for me.

"Was that Espretha?" Aloora asked innocently. She had clearly been listening to the conversation.

I nodded, "I forgot to cancel our training session this morning. She was pretty pissed."

"How's it going with her?" my friend's question was pointed.

"OK I guess. I'm certainly getting fitter," I sighed, "Look, if you don't want me to see her…"

"No, no, it's fine. She was actually nice to me when she kidnapped me. Not like the other elf. Plus she's cooperating fully with the MLO now, so that's good. It's better that we know where she is and what she's doing. I'd be interested in meeting her now she's left the cult…"

"Wait, am I a mole for you?"

"Mole?! How many crime shows do you watch? Anyway, if you're going to be a furry animal, I'd say you're more of a hamster," she joked.

I was glad she sounded more like herself, but a bit indignant at being compared to a chubby rodent with fat cheeks, "Hamster?! They bite you know!" I gnashed my teeth at her in jest and she laughed.

Shaking her head, she put her headphones back on and settled back into her chair. I wriggled around, getting comfy on the woollen covering over my seat and allowed my eyes to close again.

I woke myself with a loud snort as we pulled up outside the Magical Liaison Office. I blinked as I came to then stared. Part of the road was opening. I wondered if I was dreaming as the tarmac fell down to form a ramp. Agent Jones steered the van into the hole. Dull electric lights lit a short tunnel. After a few seconds drive, she parked Dan the van in a sleek, modern garage. I gaped as I got out of the dull van. The space was huge. The walls were pristine white and there was a large screen at one end. Complicated symbols swirled across it in glowing script. At the other end were several blue crash mats. Metal shelves held boxing gloves and weapons. A red punch bag swung from the ceiling. Round targets were set into one wall. There was a crossbow bolt embedded in one of the bullseyes. I couldn't sense any magic.

I turned to stare at the Office employees. Agent Jones was smirking, "Beats trying to find a parking spot in the city."

"What's all that for?" I asked, pointing over my shoulder at the gym equipment.

Aloora grinned at me, "Training."

I don't know where I had imagined the Office trained, but it hadn't been in a state of the art basement gym cum garage. I shook my head. This was a lot to process on so little sleep. The others began walking up a winding ramp.

"What about Dot?"

"She'll be fine in the van. Best to let her sleep if we don't need her awake." Agent Jones' voice wafted down to me. I started up the ramp, and emerged in the entranceway of the Office building.

Agent Jones looked me up and down, "You did well, considering. Get home."

I shifted uncomfortably. Aloora came to my rescue by throwing me her keys, "Go on, you can go back to my place."

I thanked her and she buzzed me out. Back in the street, I looked carefully at the road. Now I knew part of the road was a trapdoor, I deliberately looked for the edges. They were subtle and cleverly hidden by painted road markings, but they were there. I glanced around. No one was standing around, staring at the entranceway. I couldn't believe that passers-by hadn't seen the van disappear underground. I'd have to ask Aloora about it later.

I didn't feel like going to Aloora's straight away so decided to head to my favourite coffee shop. Brinda gave me an appraising look as I placed my order.

"You don't look so good today,"

I glanced down. My clothes were ripped and stained after the fall through a tree and a night on the ground. Schiztz.

"Er, it's been a rough night." That was an understatement.

She waved away my card with a look of sympathy, "It's on the house."

Schiztz, she thought I was homeless. I tried to explain, blustering an explanation, but she'd already turned to the next person in line and there was a long queue. I got more sympathetic looks as I hurried out of the door.

I walked aimlessly and only realised my treacherous feet were taking me to my shop when I entered the Arcade. I paused, momentarily overcome with emotions. A shopper brushed pass me, mumbling about idiots stopping in the middle of the bloody way. I squared my shoulders and walked on deliberately.

I stood outside the wreckage of my shop. It was as burned and damp as it had been when I'd been here last. I considered ducking under the yellow tape that the Arcade's owner had put up. A figure materialised beside me, leaning calmly on the neighbouring shop's window. I turned suddenly and sighed in relief as I recognised one of Gunther's gang of kobolds. He used them for transportation and security in his business. Rumour had it that they were fiercely loyal to the dwarf and could find anything, or anyone.

"This is a right mess," the kobold didn't mince her words, her large yellow eyes watching me with interest.

I grunted agreement and took a long sip of sweet syrupy coffee.

"What you done to have mozzers after you?"

"Mozzers?"

"Mostrim, y'know, dark elves."

I looked at her in surprise. Dark elves were a myth. Bedtime stories told to scare kids into behaving. 'Don't do that or the dark elves will get you.' 'Be good or the dark elves will carry you away.' I was always amazed that dark elves would want naughty children.

"Come on, stop winding me up, can't you see I've lost my house and home?" I put on a tone of mock self-pity. Shame it was all too real.

"I'm not winding you up. My boys have been watching this place for the boss man. Definite dark elf been sniffing around. The nose never lies." She tapped the side of her pointed nose for emphasis.

"There's no dark elves left," I tried to inject my voice with certainty.

She shrugged, "There's been talk. We hear it on the street. They're around. They never really left, just went into hiding."

"Why would they want to burn down my shop?"

"Who knows? Probably wasn't the shop they was after. Best to stay out of their way. They kill first, ask questions later." I forced myself to take another sip of coffee. The kobold kept talking, changing subjects like quicksilver. "Anyway, we got everything precious out of there," she pointed a greenish hand to a mouldering army surplus bag tucked behind the broken door, "you've got some weird stuff upstairs y'know? Nothing looked valuable, but you want me to grab anything for you?"

I thought about my possessions; my bedside lamp shaped like a wizard, my sodden clothes, my superhero figurine collection, the small shelf stacked with fantasy novels. It was just stuff but it was my stuff. All ruined and completely replaceable. "Nah, it's all just rubbish really."

The kobold nodded and I got the feeling I'd passed some sort of sentimentality test. "Boss man asked me if there was anything he could do..." her yellow eyes pierced me as if she was going to memorise anything I said.

I thought while I sipped some more coffee, "Actually, there is one thing. Has he got a workshop I can use? I want to start making jewellery again, keep my hand in while the insurance claim goes through."

She tilted her head as if taking a mental note, but didn't commit to anything. "I'll ask him." She watched me pick up the canvas bag with a smirk.

"You couldn't have got a nicer bag?" I protested as an unsavoury smell I didn't want to think too much about wafted up from it.

"Didn't want anyone thinking there was valuables inside it," her smile grew wider, showing pointed teeth and making her look predatory.

I hefted the strap over my shoulder and set off. The kobold watched me go, still leaning casually on the adjoining shop front.

I slowed as the delicious smells of cooking wafted from a nearby sandwich shop. I grabbed a toasted chicken and pesto panini with a side of chips and a chocolate bar. I got more sideways looks from the patrons and decided to take my food to go. I made myself wait to open it until I'd found somewhere to sit.

I strolled to Bute Park, away from the glances of the people out for a day's shopping in the city. I looked away from the carved stone animals lining the wall that followed the pavement from Cardiff Castle to the park. The stonemason had made them realistic and threatening with glass eyes that gave them a menacing gaze. The baboon was the worst one, mouth open and long stone fangs showing.

Once away from the creatures, I relaxed and picked a spot under a large tree off the main walkways. A light breeze was causing brown and red leaves to fall gently in the shafts of sunlight. Autumn was definitely here.

As I chewed on my panini, I watched joggers run past. I idly wondered where they were going and what their lives were like. It beat dwelling on my own problems. I finished my lunch too quickly and soon only had the chocolate bar left. I savoured it, remembering that if Espretha caught me with it, she'd throw it on the ground again. I let each bite melt on my tongue before chewing slowly. It was my form of mindfulness.

After eating, I risked opening the canvas bag the kobolds had left for me. They had done a good job. Twisted metal and semi-precious stones glinted from inside. It looked like they had recovered everything of value from the wreckage. I began to imagine creating a new jewellery collection: *Rise from the ashes*. It had a nice ring to it. I'd use copper to get a flame effect and then set in red and yellow stones. I created fantastic shapes in my mind's eye: a phoenix, a dragon. Maybe I could make everything in the collection a fire charm. That would be neat, and, if my store ever burned down again, it would all survive intact.

I settled myself onto a pile of dried leaves and stretched out to enjoy my daydream. I was pretty confident no one would touch the mouldy bag but put it securely under my sturdy boots anyway. I closed my eyes. I drifted off to sleep.

I was woken by a sharp kick to the side. I blinked up, confused and in pain. "You snore, you know?"

I groaned. I recognised that voice, “Hi Espretha, you could have just shaken me awake.”

“You look like crap,” she looked me up and down before wrinkling her noise, “you smell like it too.”

I struggled to my feet, “That’s the bag.”

Her beautiful brow furrowed as she tried to work out why I was carrying something that smelled like a toilet.

“Why does your bag smell like sulphur?”

Ugh, I had forgotten about the smelly cream Aloora had plastered on me. “Dragons,” I replied simply.

The elf paled at that, reminded of her own involvement with raising the first dragon. She recovered quickly, “Doesn’t explain why you look like a hobo.”

Anger flooded through me. Anger at the culs that had burned down my shop and destroyed my home. Anger at having to live on a friend’s sofa at thirty-five. Anger at having to start from scratch. Anger at this cul for looking down on me.

“Let’s go, elf cul,” I swung hostilely with Bane. Surprised, Espretha barely dodged the blow. It was the closest I’d ever come to hitting her.

I reversed my swing, not needing to turn the blade on my double-headed axe and aimed for her side. She stepped and turned, getting inside my reach. I ducked a blow to my head and pulled Bane towards me, connecting with her back. Her eyes widened in surprise at the contact. She leapt forward, directly onto me. I crashed to the ground, landing hard on my back. She pushed me down, using her body to trap mine. I rolled, using my heavier frame and managed to turn us both on our sides. I scowled as she grinned.

"Nice job, dwarf. Now what?"

With a grunt of effort, I twisted and managed to pin her. I lifted my axe, possessed with battle rage, ready to swing it at her.

She tsked and I felt pressure against my side. She had finally drawn her bone handled knife. It was digging into my skin. I sighed, deflating along with my anger. She was out of my league.

"Yield," I ground the word out between my teeth.

She smiled again and put away her blade with a flick of her slender wrist. "Not too shabby. Nice use of surprise, but your axe isn't the best weapon when grappling."

I felt a large rain drop land on my cheek, followed by another. A traditional Welsh downpour. I moved closer to the shelter of the large tree and leaned against the trunk.

Espretha tossed me a bottle of water, "Feeling better?"

I twisted the cap and took a long drink. I nodded.

"Feels good to fight it out, right?"

I nodded again and sighed, "It's just been a really schiztz week." That about summed it up.

"Tell me about it," she let out her own sigh.

"What are you talking about? You're a gorgeous elf who got away with raising a dragon and can do anything she wants."

She looked at me with amazement, "I knew dwarves were self-centred but you take the biscuit. I'm in thrall to the

Magical Liaison Office for life for what I did, one false move and I'll be imprisoned. I've been rejected by my entire race. My own family won't talk to me. I can't even say sorry to my best friend. I don't have a job and I'm living in a crappy so-called safe-house, which I'm sure the Office made sure was the one with the biggest rat problem in the city," she finished bitterly.

"Oh schiztz, that is bad. Why didn't you say anything before?"

"I felt bad enough you nearly got killed…twice…"

"And you broke into my flat," I added.

She grimaced, "That too. When you caught me, I thought you had everything I wanted; friends, a great business. You run your life exactly how you want. I've never been able to do that. And you've got a connection with Lorandir. I really messed that up."

I shifted uncomfortably. It was the first time she'd spoken openly about her relationship with Lorandir.

"Anyway, I guess I thought that if I could give you something, like train you into a passable warrior, it might start to make amends."

I didn't know what to say, "I guess we're both up schiztz creek then."

She laughed at that, "Guess we are; it'll take longer than I thought to whip you into shape." She took a long drink then shoved her bottle into her non-descript backpack. "Fancy a run?" she cut across my protests. I thought I was getting pretty decent.

I stared at her then pointedly looked at the sheets of rain pouring out of the sky. She laughed again, "Come on, it'll wash off some of that stink."

She set off into the downpour at a jog. I grumbled as I fitted Bane back into my belt loop, picked up the disgusting canvas bag and followed her into the rain.

I asked her if she fancied a drink after I'd recovered from the run. Espretha crinkled her straight nose, "No thanks. You need a shower. But if you're not at work, we could train daily…" She avoided my gaze, as if she was afraid of what I might say.

"Sure, why not?" I was rewarded with a full on beam of a smile that brightened her face. Elves really were beautiful. She left with a bounce in her step. I staggered across the city to Aloora's place.

I only encountered one of her housemates as I entered. He audibly gagged as I walked past.

"Just going to use the shower," I felt I had to explain the stench. I had grown accustomed to it but it was clearly still powerfully strong.

"Good job too, that is pungent" he muttered under his breath.

Once in the bathroom, I realised I had nothing to wash with. I eyed up the various bottles of shower gels and shampoos that belonged to the students here. It was an eclectic mix. I guessed the organic tea tree set was Aloora's and the designer skin care brand was probably Marco's. I opened all the other bottles and sniffed. I reasoned that the strongest smell would be best to combat the sulphuric odour. The cheap supermarket-own brand lemon shower gel smelled the strongest so I used that, soaping it into a rich lather. For good measure, I used Aloora's organic stuff too. It was zingy against my skin. I washed my hair three times with three different shampoos and treated myself to the anti-frizz conditioner one of the household used a lot, if the three empty bottles were anything to go by.

Satisfied that I no longer stank, I dashed to the lounge in a scrappy, scratchy towel that was only just the right side of a decent size. I got dressed in the only spare clothes I had and went in search of a washing machine for my stained clothes. I was just helping myself to some non-bio washing powder when Aloora came in. She made a face.

"What's the matter?" I asked.

"You should have asked. I keep my washing powder in my room. We've had a few arguments about it. Steve made us hold a house meeting. I'll probably get in trouble for letting you use that one. I swear he measures how much is left," she sighed loudly, "I can't wait to get out of here. I'd better chase that estate agent for a moving date."

"How was work?" I closed the machine and chose a setting. It was an old machine and the writing had rubbed off. I hoped I picked a setting that wasn't going to shrink my new clothes.

Aloora flopped down on one of the chairs and pulled out some paperwork from her leather satchel, "A major debrief. The Elven High Council is mollified now they know what was wrong with the dragons but it's all got a bit political. I'm leaving Jones to it while I focus on the recordings. She's pissed because she wants to be at her farm."

“I can’t imagine Agent Jones on a farm.”

“I’m not sure it’s really a farm with animals and crop rotations. I think it’s more where she escapes to.”

I tried to picture Agent Jones relaxing. Nope. I couldn’t do it. She was wound tighter than Espretha’s braids. Aloora made us both a healthy salad with some sort of aromatic dressing on the side. We ate in companionable silence at the battered wooded table shoved in one corner of the kitchen. She excused herself after dinner to work on translating the recordings.

It was nice to be physically exhausted when I collapsed onto the sofa that evening. I briefly thought about turning on the TV but I was too tired. I fell asleep before my brain could whir over stolen dragon eggs and insurance claims.

Chapter 14

The following day, I forced myself to dig out copies of rental invoices and inventory sheets. I thanked my past self for dealing with everything on email and cloud servers so I didn't have to worry about paper copies destroyed in the blaze. I forwarded copies of everything to the email address the insurance company had given me. I added a list of some of my contents too, though not everything. I didn't think they'd believe that I stored all my clothes there for business reasons for example, but I figured it was plausible that I'd have an extra chair and a wizard's lamp in my shop as part of the décor. I even attached a picture of the mural Marco had painted in case that was worth something on the claim. I got an automated email back telling me to expect a response in five to ten working days. I contemplated calling them to ask if they could speed anything up. I had about three months' worth of savings in my account thanks to my Dad's prudent finance coaching, but it would take a lot longer to sort out the shop and I needed funds to tide me over until I could reopen.

As I was telling myself the company wouldn't have even opened the email within fifteen minutes, my phone rang. I glanced at the screen and saw it was Gunther. I welcomed the distraction.

"Hi there,"

"Hey Ame, how're you doing?"

"Good, good, just sent everything off for the claim." He didn't need to know about my adventures in Breconia.

"Bethan says you want a workshop space, you getting back into making are you?"

"Got to keep busy," I forced a smile into my voice, "Bethan?"

"My right-hand kobold. Anyway, I've got just the place. I'll send you the address. Be there in an hour and I'll settle you in," he hung up. My phone bleeped as the address arrived. The other side of Cardiff. I checked the bus times. I'd have to get a shift on to get there in an hour. I grabbed the mouldy bag and stuffed my tools in. After a moment's thought, I snatched up the rest of the jewellery I had managed to save from the fire and the dragon's scale. I loaded everything into the bag and prayed it would hold.

I made it, only slightly out of breath as I jogged the last fifteen minutes. Espretha's training was paying off. Gunther had sent me to a warehouse on an industrial estate out of town. Sturdy no-nonsense buildings in shades of grey and brown lined the well-worn road leading onto the estate. I wandered around, trying to make sense of the address. It seemed as if the units were randomly assigned a number and I couldn't see an order to it. Then I spotted a kobold loading a van. I jogged over and was relieved to see Unit 21 in neat metal numbers over the red door. The kobold sniffed pointedly as I approached. He scratched his neck and stared at me with interest as I gave him a half-smile and walked in.

There was a small office, where Gunther was sitting, drinking tea and barking orders into his phone. I gave him a wave and he gave me the universal sign that he'd be two minutes. I stared around the warehouse. I had never seen the inner workings of his operation before. It was well organised and busy.

To one side, pallets were stacked, their contents wrapped in opaque plastic. Another section had floor to ceiling shelves holding cardboard boxes of various sizes. A sense of magic emanated from some of them. A pack of small flying creatures, sprites or pixies I guessed, were flitting about between the shelves, retrieving boxes and placing them onto forklifts. This was more difficult than it sounds as kobolds were whizzing forklifts around like they were driving go-karts. They skidded across the aisles and executed pinpoint turns as they selected heavier pallets and moved them to a loading bay. A large lorry was parked there and orcs were hefting the heavy boxes and pallets into its dark interior. Everyone was wearing high-vis jackets in day glow yellow.

"Ho there Amethyst!" Gunther's voice boomed as he clapped a hand on my shoulder, distracting me from the organised chaos by the loading bay.

I turned and smiled at the sight of his embroidered waistcoat covered by a florescent jacket. “Hey Gunther, how’s it going?”

“Well, well. Busy, as always. But what I wanted to show you was this way.”

He handed me a high-vis jacket of my own and led me away from the shelves and pallets towards the back of the warehouse. There he had set up a number of forges in an open space. Several of them gleamed bright hot. There were figures dressed in the same bright yellow jackets melting down metals into ingots. Others were hammering the metals into twisted shapes. Near the forges were work benches where two wizened goblins were examining jewels and sorting them into piles depending on clarity, colour and carat. At another bench, a young-ish dwarf was reading a list, his glasses glinting in the forge-light. He selected a jewel from a small heap in front of him, checked the piece of paper and then muttered a word. A perfect princess-cut diamond shone in his hand. He took out a jeweller’s loupe and held the jewel up to an angle poise lamp on his table. He grunted his satisfaction and made a tick on the paper.

Gunther led me past their tables. They looked up briefly as we passed then quickly returned to their work. “Here we go, how’s this then? It’s at the end so you won’t be disturbed and there’s the best coal Errol can eat.”

The bench he showed me was sturdy with a couple of vices attached to it for holding jewellery. A polishing machine was attached to one end, switched off. A set of doming tools were stood in a custom wooden stand. There was plenty of space for me to add my own tools. “Er, actually Errol's at my Uncle's farm for now, but I should be alright with a blowtorch."

"Of course, I'll get one brought over for you. Any metals or jewels you need, you just ask Grimstock over there," he pointed out one of the goblins, who gave a small wave, "he'll sort you out and keep tally."

I nodded, "Sounds good. How much for using this space for a few months?"

Gunther scratched his chin thoughtfully, "Well it's empty at the moment see, one of my jewellers left last month, so you can use it for free…for now. If it becomes a more permanent arrangement I'll sort out a proper contract, but let's see how we go hey? I'll charge the usual rates for materials…do you need to rent any tools?"

I shook my head, thankful I had managed to rescue them from the fire, "Thanks Gunther, this is too kind."

"Nonsense! Anything for my best customer and Dafydd Haernson's daughter!"

I smiled, grateful to my father's friend, "I've brought my kit, mind if I start straight away?"

"Atta girl! Course not. Don't worry about packing up after, someone's here all day and night and no one would dare rob this place." A darker expression crossed his face. At that point a scuffle broke out between the pixies and the kobolds as they argued over the placement of a strangely shaped box. Several of the pixies were dive-bombing the kobolds, who were flapping their arms trying to protect their faces. Gunther immediately left me and began striding over to the trouble, "Cut it out you lot!"

I began unloading the bag carefully, assessing each piece as I took it out and placing it on the bench. Dad's words echoed in my ear: "There's a place for everything and everything has its place."

Once everything was unpacked, I put on my enchanting goggles and looked at the dismal pile of melted metal and blackened jewels. I'd been itching to look through them since I'd arrived. The warehouse lit up through the brown tinted lenses. Wards of all kinds sparkled across the walls. I recognised dwarven, fae and even shifter magic in the swirl of colours. The auras of the workers gleamed brightly. It was like looking through a kaleidoscope.

A slimy greenish aura detached itself from a workbench and walked towards me. I moved my goggles up as he approached. He held out a hand with long claws on each finger. I took it gingerly. I felt bones grind as he gave me a hearty handshake, "I'm Grimstock. Boss man said to make sure you have everything you need. Whatchoo need?"

"Er, I'm ok right now. Just assessing what stock I've got left."

He nodded his head in sympathy, "Heard about the fire. Bad business," he turned his head to the pile on my bench, "I'd melt it all down if I was you. Not sure if those stones will have survived the heat either."

His gloomy assessment was probably right, but it made me bristle a bit. I kept silent. I couldn't risk annoying Gunther's employees with snide remarks.

"Now what's this then?" his eyes alighted on the bright dragon's scale with interest. He reached out and before I could stop him, the scale was in his clawed hands. He turned it over and over between long mottled fingers. “Don’t see magic like this every day…where’d you get this from then?”

“Found it,” I was deliberately vague.

His eyes narrowed. I wasn’t sure if it was suspicion or respect, “Rightchoo are then. Well, you let me know if I can do anyfink for you.”

He returned to his own station stiffly and began sorting through gemstones again. I sifted through my own pile, separating it into pieces that were intact – thank you fire charms! - metal that I would need to melt to work with and stones that I’d need to clean before I could assess if they were damaged.

With a sigh, I got out my handheld dremel polisher and plugged it in. I set to work cleaning up all the gems so I could decide what was usable. After a few hours, I was surprised that most of the stones were alright. Only one or two had blackened beyond repair. I glanced at my phone to check the time and was surprised to see a message from Aloora telling me to call her.

I looked up the bus times and, with a hasty thanks to Gunther and Grimstock, left to catch the next one. I took Gunther at his word that my gear would be safe. Once safely on board, I called my friend.

“What’s happened?” It said a lot about my life recently that I automatically assumed something was wrong.

“Only the most exciting thing this year!”

I reflected on that. Over the past year my friend had been kidnapped and I'd seen three dragons raised. Aloora ploughed on, "You'll never guess!"

"What is it?"

"Guess!"

I sighed heavily and thought about my friend, "You've translated the recordings and dinner's on you tonight?"

"No! Guess again!"

"You've got another ten thousand subscribers on your channel and dinner's on you tonight?"

"Nowhere near!"

This game could go on all day. "What then?!"

A man in a flat cap got on the bus and, despite a plethora of empty seats, chose to sit behind me breathing down my neck. I glared at him. He just grinned and took a swig from a battered hip flask. I guessed it wasn't water. I got up and moved away, listening to Aloora.

"We've only gone and been invited to *the* event of the year! Everyone who's anyone will be there and we're invited! I can't wait! I've only seen pictures…"

"Slow down, who's been invited to where?"

"To the Equinox Ball…" she sensed my blank stare down the phone, "…the elven Equinox Ball…in Breconia!"

"Didn't we just get back from there?"

"The city not the reservation silly, and it's not until next week but the Council sent a message by gryphgeon so it's real. I've got the invite here, where are you?!"

"Gunther leant me a space in his warehouse."

“You know what this means don’t you?” I groaned inwardly as she answered her own question, “Shopping! Now get back here, I want to show you the invite. Dinner’s on me!”

I lifted my head back and let out the sigh I’d been holding in. Schiztz, I hated shopping and I’d never been to a ball before. Did a ball mean there would be dancing? Schiztz. My education had been distinctly lacking in any dancing. Then another thought struck me. Lorandir was back in Breconia, I’d get to see him again. I didn’t know if I was happy or nervous or both about that.

Chapter 15

Aloora was practically bouncing off the walls when I walked in the door. She thrust a piece of thick card into my hands. Golden patterns swirled around the edges in the shape of climbing vines. One side had a tree with a crown looped around the trunk. The symbol of the Elven High Council. The other side had an ivy leaf stamped at the top and fancy gold writing underneath. I had to tilt it in the hall lighting to make out the words:

Ms Amethyst Haernson is cordially invited to the annual Equinox Ball on the Twenty Second of September.

RSVP

"The gryphgeon is waiting for your reply, I've already sent mine in!"

I looked down at a small catlike creature sitting regally in the student hallway. I had never seen one of the elven messengers before. It looked like a cross between a sleek cat and a small hawk. Its golden colouring was at odds with the chipped wallpaper. It sensed my gaze and turned its head my way, flicking its long tail around its feet. The back set were feline while the front set were definitely bird feet with pointed talons. Its sharp orange eyes rested on me and it opened its curved beak before turning away to peck at the spot where its fur and feathers met on its back around its wing joints. Not so regal after all. I lifted my gaze back to my friend.

"OK, but the twenty second of September is a week away, that's not a lot of time…"

She waved away my concerns, "It's all sorted. The entire Office team has been invited. We're going up in the morning, so we'll have the whole day to explore then the ball then come home after breakfast the following day. There was another note confirming accommodation. I've persuaded Agent Jones that as it's official business, we can have tomorrow afternoon to shop!"

I groaned, "You know I hate shopping." It was only a half protest as I was starting to get excited. If we had the whole day to explore, perhaps I could talk to the elven smith who had been able to merge two types of magic into one piece so it could be found by the wearer.

"I'll help, it'll be fun!"

"Fine!"

My friend beamed at me excitedly then led me into the kitchen. She began preparing another salad but, as a treat, added a crispy part-bake baguette to the side. I slathered it with the sunflower oil spread she used instead of butter.

After dinner, she went off to update her social media channels, still buzzing about the invite. I decided to call Mum and Dad. I tried a video call first, not expecting them to pick up. Unbelievably, they answered first ring.

"Hi there!" they beamed. Their faces were flushed and, was that steam rising up in the background?

"Er, I can call back later if you're busy…"

Mum laughed, "No, no, we've just had a hot tub installed and we're trying it out." She waved a glass of wine towards the camera. Condensation dripped down the glass.

"It's great for sore muscles, I should have got one of these years ago!" Dad chimed in, "You can have a go when you next come over."

I bit my lip and grunted. Mum gave Dad a playful swat on his shoulder, "Now how are you love?"

"Did you sort the insurance?" Classic Dad.

I nodded, "Yep, I've sent everything in, just waiting for them to reply."

"And you're alright for money?"

"Fine Dad. I've got a bit saved and Gunther's letting me use one of his work benches…"

"Good, good, straight back to it hey Ame!"

I ploughed on, trying to reassure them I was fine "And the Magical Liaison Office are paying me for some freelance work…"

"You're not fighting dragons again are you?" Mum's eyes narrowed.

I silently cursed the social media footage and newspaper articles that meant almost all of my dragon encounters were documented, "Not exactly…more consulting." That sounded better than being dropped onto a tree by a large creature and fighting crazy elves. Emboldened, I pressed on, "In fact, I've been invited to the Equinox Ball in Breconia!"

"Oh Ame, that's amazing! What are you wearing?"

Schiztz, of course Mum would be interested in that, "Er, well, all my clothes were pretty much destroyed and I didn't really have a ball gown anyway, so Aloora's taking me to find something."

"Fabulous! When are you going, I'll come too. I fancy some shopping in the city."

Double schiztz. I tried to put her off, "We're going tomorrow actually, so it's a bit short notice. I'll send a picture when I've found something…"

"Nonsense, I'll set off in the morning, meet you for lunch then we'll get going."

"Won't Dad mind?" I tried.

He laughed, "No, no, I'll enjoy the peace! Plus I'll get to watch what I want on the telly."

"That's settled then, I'll call you when I've parked."

"Sounds good Mum. So, hot tubs aside, what else have you been up to?"

"Well, you know Jenny? She…"

I never heard what Jenny had done because Mum dropped the phone into the hot tub. The screen went mercifully dark before I could get a clear view of the bottom half of my parents. I hung up and left them to the painful and often fruitless task of trying to dry out a smartphone.

Next up I messaged my Uncle. I immediately got back three photos of Errol: one of him sleeping with all four legs in the air, one of him breathing a jet of fire and another of him begging for a piece of Welsh coal. I smiled and sent back a string of emoji happy faces and a heart.

Marco came and joined me in the sitting room. He poured me a glass of wine as he flicked on the TV and changed channels until he found a soap opera that he liked. Sometimes he was really good at being quiet. As the catchy theme music played, I pulled out a blank pad of paper I had borrowed from Aloora and began sketching some designs. I kept that up for about an hour before a Midsomer Murder episode came on the TV. Marco and I watched two of the long episodes back to back before finally heading to bed.

Chapter 16

Morning arrived with an excitable gnome pulling my eyes open, "I'm heading into work – come get me at lunchtime and we'll find some dresses!"

"Ugh, what time is it? No, wait, I think Mum's coming shopping too!" My bleary brain was struggling to catch up.

"Great, I love your Mum and she's got good taste! See you later," Aloora bounded out of the room and I heard the door slam. That woke some of her housemates who I heard begin to surface for their lectures.

I rushed to get ready before the students descended. I texted my Dad to find out what was happening with Mum. I got a call back from Mum. Her voice sounded far away and I heard traffic in the background. She said she was using Dad's phone and named one of the upmarket pizza chain restaurants in Cardiff for lunch. She hung up quickly as a squeal of brakes sounded in the background. I stared at my phone and hoped she was OK. I texted Aloora the restaurant name and headed to Gunther's warehouse with my sketches. Gunther wasn't in his office and one of his kobold team said he'd gone to meet a client. I gave a nod hello to Grimstock and his companions before settling at my bench. I got straight to work and lost myself in coaxing the metal and gemstones to respond to my tools and form my designs.

After a little while, a loud clapping broke into my concentration. I looked up and pushed back my enchanting goggles. An orc was clapping loudly and laughing at a scuffle between the pixies and kobolds. The noise echoed across the warehouse. Even the goblins were laughing. One kobold was trying to break up the fight, her voice adding to the cacophony of noise. A young dwarf got up from his crafting bench and walked over, gesturing violently with a pickaxe.

As I grinned at the spectacle, inspiration struck me. What if the unlosable jewellery I wanted to make could be found by making a noise? Then it wouldn't matter about merging magical signatures. I was excited. As the fight broke up, I turned back to my bench and began experimenting on one of the few bracelets that had been left intact after the fire.

After about an hour, a polite cough broke into my concentration. I looked up into Gunther's beaming face. Next to him, his kobold lieutenant. Bethan, leered at me.

"Glad to see you're making yourself at home!" Gunther boomed over the background noise in the warehouse.

"Thanks Gunther, it's great. Look, I've finally made some progress on unlosable jewellery," I clapped my hands twice and the bracelet in front of me emitted a series of notes.

He bent down to look at the piece, "Very nice." Then he cocked his head, "Is that the Superman theme tune?"

I grinned and nodded.

"Very good. Clap on, clap off! Now anyone who breaks in just has to clap and they know where the valuables are kept. Nice idea," the kobold grinned at me nastily.

Schiztz. I hadn't even thought of that. My pride deflated, "I could change the activation sound. It doesn't have to be claps…"

"So the burglars would have to torture people to find out the activation noise. That's dark Haernson," Bethan was enjoying ripping my idea to shreds.

I clapped again to turn the noise off and pushed the bracelet away, "Are you here for a reason?" I asked the kobold pointedly.

Gunther stepped in to deescalate the hostility, "Bethan found Master Ironfist at your shop…"

"He was lurking around," she interrupted, "so I asked what he wanted and he said he needed to talk to you. So I called Gunther and he invited him over." She pointed towards the office with another grin.

"Yes, yes, thank you Bethan. It's a real honour that the Council want to talk to you Ame. Do you want to use my office?"

The kobold sensed I wasn't too happy about this and smirked, "An honour unless she's been doing something she doesn't want the Council to know about."

I narrowed my eyes at her. Gunther interrupted again, "Alright, thank you. Don't you have something to oversee? I'm not paying you to wind up my customers!"

She wandered off to the loading bay, still smirking. I felt I had to reassure Gunther, “I’m not doing anything wrong. Thank you, I’d love to use your office.”

I followed him across the concrete floor trying to project a confidence I didn’t feel. Last time I had seen Ironfist, he had wanted to take my axe.

He seemed much less intimidating in Gunther’s cramped office and rose from the wheeled chair to shake my hand as I entered.

“Thank you for seeing me Ms Haernson. I was most distraught to hear about the fire at your shop. A bad business,” he shook his head in sympathy.

“No security today?” I raised an eyebrow and folded my arms. I wasn’t trusting this sudden change in attitude.

“I’ll leave you to it, shall I?” Gunther exited hastily and bustled over to supervise his employees.

“Would you like to shut the door Ms Haernson?” the Council member sat back down on the chair and made himself comfortable. He smoothed his long, plaited beard down and adjusted the cuffs of his smart suit delicately.

I shut the door and turned back, ready for an argument. I waited for him to speak first. I wanted to know what the fight was about before saying something I might regret. The Dwarven Arms Council wasn’t an organisation you wanted to make an enemy of if you didn’t have to.

“Now, this is a very unusual visit for me, I must say,” he began, “It’s not often that a dwarf is invited to the elven city, much less to attend the Equinox Ball…”

“How do you know about that?” I gaped.

He smiled, looking like a clerk who's just solved a difficult sum. "We have our ways," he replied, not giving anything away. "You may not be aware, but this is the first time a dwarf has been invited to the ball in five hundred years. This is very exceptional, see?"

I looked at him blankly. That was a long time, but I had no idea where this was going.

"So, you see, it's very important that the dwarf attending is an excellent representative for dwarfkind."

I blinked at him, "What?"

"Naturally, we take an interest in our representative, so I will be ensuring you are suitably presented and escorted."

"Suitably presented and escorted. What does that mean?"

"Well, see," he coughed and had the good grace to look a little uncomfortable under my stare, "we, that is to say I, will be overseeing your attire and I will be formally requesting that I accompany you…"

I snorted in protest.

"I don't think you fully understand…"

I interrupted him sharply "Oh I think I understand. Let me get this straight: a few days ago you were in my shop, telling me I wasn't a full dwarf and now you want me to represent all dwarves at a ball? Is that about right?"

He shifted in his seat, "Your grasp of the situation is blunt. So allow me to be equally blunt. Relations between dwarves and elves are strained at best. This is an opportunity to build bridges. An opportunity the Council does not want to pass up."

I bit my lip, considering.

"We would not dream of asking you to do this without compensation…" he let that hang there.

I raised an eyebrow sceptically, "Like what?"

"Well of course we would pay for your outfit…"

"In exchange for vetoing what I wear."

Unperturbed, he carried on, "…and we are prepared to consider the question of your dwarfishness."

I blinked. This was a big deal. The Dwarven Arms Council were notoriously purist. "And my axe?"

"We will make no further attempts to remove Bane from your custody…unless you start killing dwarves. Well, what do you say?"

My first instinct was to tell him to shove his deal. I decided to be more mature so took a moment to think. They wanted me more than I wanted them. I wondered how far I could push this, "You will pay for my outfit and my friend's outfit, including accessories."

He nodded.

"You will not veto my outfit choices. Only my best friend or Mum can do that."

He pursed his lips. I continued, "I don't want you to consider my dwarfishness."

His mouth dropped open. He couldn't believe anyone would reject the chance to be considered a full dwarf, under the protection and jurisdiction of the Council. I held up my hand to stop his protest, "It's not fair that you consider it for me just because of an invite to a party. If you're going to consider me a full dwarf, you have to extend that to all half-dwarves."

“That is preposterous!” he blurted out. He narrowed his eyes at me, “You are being difficult Ms Haernson.”

I shrugged, “Maybe. But you’re the ones who are all about the letter of the law. How can you justify making an exception for one person?”

He shifted uncomfortably at that, “I don’t have the authority to agree to that.”

“OK, what can you agree to?”

He thought for a moment, stroking his beard, “I can promise that I will raise the matter at the next full Council meeting. I should warn you it is unlikely they will agree. However, the laws are old and perhaps worth reconsidering. In the meantime, as a representative of the Council and all dwarves, you will be under our protection and, if you choose, you can have certain rights granted to you.”

“Such as?”

“The right to call your products ‘dwarfmade’.”

I inhaled sharply. This was a huge concession. I had never heard of it being granted to a half breed before. It meant I could increase my prices for sure, and advertise my dwarfishness. But it also meant I would be subject to quality inspections with fines if I wasn’t meeting their standards. “Let’s say I accept your offer. What do you want me to do at this ball?”

He waved away my suspicions, “Nothing you wouldn’t be doing already. Eat, drink, dance. Have a good time. It will be enough that you are present.”

“So all I have to do is go to the ball with you as an escort and you’ll pay for mine and Aloora’s clothes and make sure my ownership of Bane isn't questioned again and treat me like a full dwarf. What am I missing?"

"You are missing nothing. As I said, relations with the elves are strained. This would be a huge step towards making them more…friendly. Will you do it?" he looked at me earnestly.

I bit my lip and thought of the good it could do, not just for me but for all dwarves and half-dwarves. "Alright."

He leapt to his feet and clasped my wrist in the traditional dwarven gesture. A deal had been sealed.

"I'm going shopping this afternoon. I guess you can come, as you're paying."

He beamed, "Excellent."

We left Gunther's office and made our way back into town. One thing I'll say for the Council is that they travel in style. A plush chauffeur driven car was waiting outside Gunther's warehouse. I climbed inside, getting comfortable on the leather seats. A mini fridge held bottles of water, juice and what I took to be bottles of strong dwarf-brewed beer. Ironfist pressed a button and soothing classical music played through the speakers.

The driver dropped us as close to the pizza restaurant Mum had chosen for lunch as he could before driving off sedately until he was needed again. This was a different life to city buses and walking everywhere. Aloora and Mum were already at the restaurant and reacted with surprise when I arrived with Ironfist in tow. I made the introductions quickly as I sensed Mum was about to ask if we were an item. She was very impressed to learn he was a member of the Council and very excited when I mentioned he was paying for our outfits. The conversation was stilted and quickly turned to shopping plans. I let Aloora and Mum rattle through the shops they wanted to go to and the best order to visit them to get the most out of the trip. I helped myself to the warm breadsticks.

Ironfist interrupted their conversation with a polite cough, "I wonder if I could venture a suggestion." Mum and Aloora were too polite to say anything but their looks clearly said that his input wasn't welcome. "I think it would be best to try Madam Tinselle's first."

Mum inhaled sharply, "You don't mean the Madam Tinselle? But she deals in haute couture!"

Even I had heard of the famous fashion designer based here in the city. I stopped eating bread as my mouth fell open. Her designs were often seen at film premieres and other red carpet events.

Ironfist nodded, "It is *the* Equinox Ball. Couture is appropriate."

"Don't you need an appointment for her shop?" Aloora chimed in, trying not to seem too excited.

Ironfist shrugged as if he dealt with celebrity fashion designers every day, "She will see us, I'm sure."

Mum actually squealed and quickly began drilling Ironfist on how he knew Madam Tinselle. As the pizzas arrived, they began talking about which celebrities had been wearing her gowns.

Madame Tinselle's shop was a discreet boutique opposite Cardiff Castle. I wondered if she was annoyed at the banging noises coming from behind the castle walls as the repairs to fix the damage the red dragon had caused were well underway.

Ironfist pressed the brass buzzer confidently and informed the female voice who answered who he was.

"One moment please," she replied. Seconds later, she was back, "Please come in, Madame Tinselle will be happy to attend you."

He pushed the dark, green door open and ushered us through with a bow. I self-consciously wiped the soles of my heavy leather boots on the welcome mat before stepping onto the rich, blue, deep pile carpet. A tall, willowy blonde lady smiled and told us that Madame would be "right down". She gestured at a couple of low, squashy sofas close to the window. I sat down cautiously. I sank into the soft cushions. I kept one hand on the arm of the sofa so I could get myself back to my feet. Mum perched on the edge of the seat, her handbag on her lap, a nervous smile playing on her lips. Aloora was fighting with a huge cushion to get some space on the sofa. Ironfist wisely stayed standing.

There wasn't a single clothes rail in this shop. Instead, three mannequins held samples of Madame's wares. A further dress swung from a picture rail, looking more like a piece of art than clothing. A crystal chandelier hung from the ceiling, reflecting the light around the room. A curved staircase with a golden bannister descended towards the back of the shop. Behind it, a rich velvet blue curtain hung on a golden rail, screening the back of the shop from view. A triptych of full-length mirrors in front of a small stool completed the shop, creating their own corner.

The shop worker floated over with a silver tray of champagne flutes brimming with bubbly liquid. I took one and held it carefully. Madame Tinselle descended slowly down the curved staircase. I took a sip of champagne as she glided towards us. She was wearing a plum dress that seemed to shimmer as it caught the flattering lighting.

“Good Afternoon and bienvenue – welcome – to my humble shop,” she held out a hand to me. I took it gently then sneezed as her strong perfume tickled my nose. Mum rolled her eyes and handed me a tissue. I used it, muttering apologies. My cheeks heated as Madame retrieved a lacy handkerchief from a pocket somewhere in her dress and dabbed at her own hand. Her assistant rushed over with a small bottle of anti-bacterial hand gel. Madame used it pointedly. She moved onto Mum, who gushed, “It’s an honour to be here.”

Madame beamed at that and continued onto Aloora. When she got to Ironfist she kissed him once on each cheek. I wondered how exactly they knew each other.

“To what do I owe ze honour of such esteemed guests?” she asked. Her bright eyes scanning across us.

“These two lovely young ladies have been invited to the Equinox Ball,” he started.

“Magnifique! How fabulous! A dwarf invited to an elven Ball! But - naughty, naughty - zat is less than a week away.”

“Yes, the first dwarves to attend in hundreds of years…ah, well. Of course, if you can’t help then we can go elsewhere…I’m sure we can get something off the rack…”

he feigned disappointment and took a step towards the door.

Madam clasped a hand to her heart in horror, “I didn’t say I could not do it. I said it was less than a week away!” With her mind made up, she bustled into action. Her silk skirt rustled as she clapped her hands at her assistant. “Measurements!” she cried, “You first!” She pointed a thick finger at me.

I used the arm of the sofa to push myself upwards and followed where she gestured to the stool in front of the mirrors. I looked around for help. Madam flicked her fingers, “Climb onto the step, quick quick, we cannot waste one moment!”

I stepped onto the low stool and stared at the mirrors. It wasn’t often I stood in front of a full length mirror, let alone three of them. My frizzy reddish brown hair formed a strange halo around my face. My brown eyes stared back at me three times.

“Hmmm,” Madame was walking around me, squinting. She clicked her fingers and her assistant handed her a measuring tape. “Arms out,” she ordered. I obeyed and she began taking measurements. I felt my cheeks heat as she shouted them out to her assistant, who noted them down in a fluffy notebook.

Once she was satisfied with the inches, she began holding up swatches of fabric by my face, “You have a very pale complexion…” it didn’t sound like a compliment, “…and such dark eyes…” I fought the instinct to shut my eyes, “so many colours will make you look washed out…”

It felt like ages as she discarded one swatch after another. Eventually she settled on a deep red and shouted a number to her assistant. “Now, shoes! Please remove…zose,” she struggled to place a name to my gothic style leather boots.

I crouched down and awkwardly removed the boots. Her assistant appeared with a stack of shoeboxes. One by one, she held out the left shoe and placed it on my foot. Madame narrowed her eyes and considered each piece of footwear. Some had heels so high, I was worried I’d break my neck if I wore them. Luckily Madame instinctively rejected those. She shouted out more instructions to her assistant, “Two inch heel, closed toe!” Then she turned to Aloora, “Now you,” she gestured.

I stepped down from the stool, grabbed my boots and headed back to the sofa. I sank down with relief.

“Do you think she’d sign something for me?” Mum asked, clearly awestruck.

“Maybe,” I had no idea. My mind was still reeling from my first custom dress experience. I don’t know what I had expected, but it hadn’t been this. I’d been manhandled, measured and had my curves shouted out for everyone to hear.

Aloora was subjected to the same treatment, but it seemed to be finished in half the time. Probably because she’s half my size, I thought glumly. Then Madame was done.

“I will have your dresses ready. I send direct to Breconia. I assume you are staying at ze palace. Ze usual account Monsieur?”

Ironfist nodded, beaming at her.

“Er, don’t we need a fitting or something?” I asked, ignorant of the ways of couture.

She gave me an offended look, “Non, non! I will make zese dresses for you and zey will fit like a glove! Anuzzer fitting indeed! Humph!”

Ironfist soothed her while I mumbled apologies and backed towards the door. Mum was glaring daggers at me. Ironfist managed to placate Madam and she gave him another kiss on each cheek as we left.

Mum seemed to bc weighing something up. “Can I have your autograph please?” she burst out. Madame laughed and instead whirled a silk scarf from one of the mannequins. Her assistant produced a fabric pen from somewhere and handed it to Madame. The designer signed it with a flourish and presented it to Mum. Then we were back outside in the slight chill of the September air.

Chapter 17

The day we were scheduled to travel to the ball arrived quickly. I had spent all my time at my workbench in Gunther's warehouse and only travelled back to Aloora's place to sleep. Aloora was working long hours at the Magical Liaison Office as they prepared for the Ball and Marco was busy with set design for a local production of the *Lysistrata.* I had no desire to spend more time with her other, more hostile, housemates than necessary.

In the weak morning sunlight, I packed some overnight things into a small backpack I had borrowed from Aloora. I was already dressed in the best of the clothes I'd hastily bought after my shop had been burned down. This meant a pair of dark jeans and a t-shirt with cogs stretched tight over my chest. I shrugged on my red leather jacket, miraculously undamaged. Then I went to find Aloora. I knocked gently on her door. My best friend was not normally an early riser. True to form, she was still fast asleep. I shook her shoulder then turned on the lights. She squirreled herself away under the covers.

"Five more minutes...."

“Don’t make me throw a glass of water over you! Come on, you’ve been raving about this bloody ball all week.”

She peeked her head out and swore at me before heaving herself out of bed. She got dressed carefully in a striped dress before selecting her costume jewellery. I thought of the present I had made her in my bag. I almost gave it to her then to stop her from draping on another strand of oversized pearls, but thought it would be better to do it just before the ball started. I wasn’t good at dealing with emotions and I didn’t know how she’d react for sure to a genuine dragon scale collar.

We shouldered our bags and walked to the Office in the city centre. There were no chauffeurs for us today. Aloora was the designated driver and hadn’t been allowed to take the van home overnight.

The sentient door knocker was snoozing as Aloora buzzed us in and then led the way down the steps to the garage. Dot was already leaning on the van, bundled up as ever in a thick woollen jumper. This one was a deep sapphire colour and she had a contrasting orange scarf.

“Agent Jones not here?” I asked. I was surprised, I’d expected her to be the first one here.

Dot gave a mischievous smile, “She’s not coming.”

“What?” Aloora’s mouth dropped open, “What’s so important she’s missing the Equinox Ball?”

Dot shrugged, “She said she’d prefer to spend more time at the farm.”

There was something I was missing here. I furrowed my brow as I tried to figure it out. Aloora opened the van and threw her backpack into the back. Then she squealed. I hurried over. She was handling two fabric bags reverently. They were emblazoned with Madame Tinselle's name. My friend started to unzip one. I shook my head and put my backpack inside, avoiding the dress protectors.

Dot swatted her hand away, "We've got to get going. You can admire your dresses when we get there."

"Just one little look. I just want to touch it," pleaded Aloora.

Dot shook her head, "Don't make me call Jones. She won't be happy to be called away from her rest and relaxation." The vampire made it sound like an innuendo as she slammed the door authoritatively and got into the van.

"What?" I had definitely missed something.

Aloora got in the driver's seat and cranked up the music. An epic fantasy soundtrack blared out from the speakers. Dot got herself comfortable before pulling out her sunglasses to cover her eyes. I strapped Bane into one of the weapons spots the van had, next to a couple of crossbows that seemed to be the Office's weapon of choice.

Aloora pressed a button on the van's dashboard and the garage door set into the tarmac of the road above us swung down. I pressed my face to the window, trying to see more of how the mechanism worked. I barely got a glimpse as Aloora put her foot down. The tyres squealed and we raced up the ramp and onto the Cardiff streets. It was early enough to avoid traffic and we left the city quickly. My body was warring between feeling sick from Aloora's aggressive driving and sleepy from the warm interior of the van.

“What’s this about Agent Jones?” I asked the vampire. In answer, I got a snore from Dot who was managing to sleep as Aloora overtook slow lorries on winding roads. I gave up. I did not want to distract my friend from her driving. The high-topped vehicle wobbled dangerously every time we turned a corner.

After a long, stomach-churning ride, we finally arrived at Breconia about the same time that the morning rush hour was getting into full swing back in Cardiff. The same pale mist crept up to envelop us, but I couldn’t feel any menacing magical auras this time. We breezed through and were ushered along the road by elves dressed in silver. They would have looked regal except they were carrying those lollipop paddles that ushers use in car parks to direct drivers to spaces. One of them directed us to a spot, looking distinctly unimpressed by Dan the van. I was tempted to activate the rune to set it alight just to watch his snooty face, but decided against it.

I tried to wake Dot up. It’s pretty hard to wake a sleeping vampire in the daytime. I tried a combination of shaking her hard and shouting her name. Aloora watched my efforts with amusement before pulling out a silver crossbow bolt from the glovebox. She waved it vaguely towards the sleeping vampire, who awoke with a start.

“Ugh,” Dot rubbed her eyes, “You could have used the garlic at least.”

Aloora shrugged, “Couldn’t find it in the glove box, sorry.”

I blinked at them stupidly.

Dot pulled herself out of her seat, adjusting her scarf so it was wrapped in an elegant knot around her neck. “It’s a natural self-defence thing. Garlic’s a lot less intrusive though, doesn’t make me feel like I’m about to be killed,” she glared at the back of Aloora’s head.

“I didn’t know the garlic thing was real,” I mumbled.

“Oh, it’s not really. Any strong smell will do. Blood preferably, but no one likes carrying that around in the van. Jones bought the garlic as a joke I think, but it works.”

“Right,” I didn’t know what else to say.

“Shall we see where stuffed shirt over there wants us to go now?” she pointed out of the window at one of the elves who was standing to attention outside the van. He was sweating slightly and looked nervous. A couple of cat sized gryphgeons circled his feet. I couldn’t read animal minds but they looked like they were plotting to trip him up.

I unhooked Bane from the restraints and exited. His eyes rolled back in his head when he saw the weapon.

“Miss, um, it’s no weapons allowed,” he said nervously.

I looked at him and decided to stretch the truth, “I’m a dwarf. It’s a cultural piece, not a weapon.”

“Um, I really don’t think…”

Ironfist stepped from his chauffeur driven car in time to hear the exchange, “Master Ironfist, representative of the Dwarven Arms Council at your service.” He bowed slightly to the elf. “Ms Haernson is also here as our representative and, as she’s already said, it is indeed cultural for dwarves to retain their symbolic tools in such situations.”

This was clearly above the elf's paygrade, "OK, um, but you'll have to sign it in when you get to the city. This way, please."

I mouthed "thank you" to Ironfist who inclined his head in acknowledgement. I slung my backpack over one shoulder and Aloora's over the other. She was struggling with the dress bags but wouldn't let me take one from her. We followed the elf towards the edge of the valley.

The elf turned and saw us carrying our bags, "Please, we will see to it that your bags are taken to your rooms."

I shook my head, "I'm alright with my bag, but she might need some help." I looked over at Aloora. He rushed over to help her but she refused to give up the designer bags. In the end Dot persuaded her to let someone help so they didn't get creased or dropped. The vampire easily carried them, cradling them in her arms with her own less ostentatious dress bag. She had her own overnight bag hooked over her forearm. It was a strange tapestry style bag that I imagined was used in Victorian times. I briefly wondered how old Dot was. Then I looked up. The valley was as majestic as the last time we were here. Hazy autumn sunlight streamed down, adding an air of mysticism to the view. The dark forest stretched away on the other side of the valley. I wondered how all the dignitaries would make it down there in their smart shoes and fancy clothes.

I soon had my answer. The elf explained that there were two options to get to the city of Breconia, deep within the woods. We could be escorted via gryphons or use a portal that had been set up especially for the ball.

I looked at the large golden creatures pawing at the ground as they waited for their passengers. I shuddered as I remembered my last flight. Aloora was torn between the allure of the flying animals and making sure the outfits were safe. Dot saved her by saying she would take the dresses via the portal. She stepped through without a second's hesitation.

Aloora took her backpack from me and was already walking towards the gryphons. I wasn't sure I liked this new reckless streak in my friend.

"No way! I'm taking the portal."

"Suit yourself, you're missing all the fun!" she grinned back at me.

I shook my head and headed towards the portal, trying to avoid stepping on any of the gryphgeons who were winding themselves around the legs of anyone who stayed still for too long. It shimmered in the weak sunshine. I felt the elven magical energy surrounding it. Opalescent colours swirled across it, masking the destination from view. I had never travelled by portal before. I was still hesitating when Ironfist clasped my elbow and propelled me forward.

"Never look weak in front of the elves!" he whispered as we crossed through.

There was a strange sucking sensation and a feeling of falling sideways. I couldn't see anything except pale rainbows. My head reeled as the sensation was coupled with imprints of a forest as the elven magic took hold. In less than a second, I was stumbling onto a genuine forest floor. I took a second to get my balance back. Ironfist seemed equally disorientated and a guard had to usher us to one side so the next visitors could get through.

As the forest swam into focus, I gasped. We were in a large airy clearing. A stream babbled through and pooled in a beam of sunlight. The water bounced the light into small rainbows as it played over smooth pebbles. Some elven children were running across it, chided by their parents as they scurried out of the way of guests. Several paths meandered away from the clearing into a well-maintained forest. Any leaves had been swept to one side to keep the soft, mossy paths clear. The paths curved through the forest, gracefully carving a route around the trees. Shafts of sunlight beamed through the foliage, creating a pattern of light on the mossy floor. The trees themselves were huge. Red and brown wooden trunks reached towards the sky. I followed them upwards to the canopy of greens and golds. The leaves seemed to shiver in a light breeze, lending an air of movement to the still woods. Some of the foliage was beginning to turn to autumn colours and I caught glimpses of bright reds and burnt oranges. In a word, it was breath-taking.

I caught movement from one of the tree trunks and stared. Winding staircases made of thick vines were twisted around each large trunk. Elves were walking up and down the trees on different flights of steps and disappearing into the trees through doorways that looked like knots in the trunks. As I followed one group of elves ascending, I noticed another pair walking along a vine bridge that connected two trees together just below the canopy. I gulped. None of the vine bridges had guardrails.

Ironfist was gazing around with as much wonder as me, although he was trying to appear indifferent beneath his immaculately groomed and plaited beard. "It's got nothing on the mines of Jarnstradr," he named the ancient dwarven underground city.

I smiled. I'd only been to Jarnstradr once when Dad had insisted I get a feel for my culture. It was impressive, true, but in an entirely different and deeper, more underground, sort of way than this forest city.

Another elf with orange paddle sticks was gesturing frantically at the sky and three gryphons landed gracefully to one side of the clearing. Aloora was on one of them. She slid off its back and bounded over to us with a huge smile on her face.

"That was ace! You should have tried it!"

"The portal was enough excitement for me," I responded with feeling.

"Where to now?" asked Dot, peering round. Everyone else seemed to be being led somewhere by busy-looking elves with their equivalent of clipboards – large round leaves with writing scrawled on them in Elvish script.

I peered around the clearing. The majority of the groups were heading down the broadest path, accompanied by elves in green or grey uniforms. A troupe of mounted gryphon riders were leading their animals in the opposite direction towards the clearing, picking their way carefully past the guests. I pointed, "I guess we go that way."

I started to turn but my foot got caught on the trailing dress bag that Dot was carrying. I stumbled and fell to the ground. I let out a small cry of surprise as I fell. Instantly, all eyes turned to me, sprawled out on the floor.

"Sorry," Dot grimaced.

The soft moss had broken my fall and I was more embarrassed than hurt. I turned bright red as I pushed myself upright. "Don't even worry about it," I reassured her. Everyone else was still looking at me, feasting on my embarrassment. "All good here, nothing to see, I'm fine," I said cheerily, raising my voice to be heard. I guess I was going to be staring at the floor for the entire visit to avoid meeting anyone's gaze.

As we started to move, the gryphon riders intercepted us.

"It is a little way to the palace, I thought you might appreciate a ride," a familiar voice said. I looked up and up, past the large gryphon and into Lorandir's handsome face. Schiztz. He had definitely seen me fall on my face. I felt my cheeks begin to heat again.

"It's OK thanks, we'll walk," I replied stubbornly.

"Speak for yourself!" Aloora cut in, already striding towards the largest gryphon.

"Here, come on, Finn is lovely really," the elf tried to reassure me. He did something with the reins and the beast tucked its front legs down onto the ground so I could mount it more easily.

I squinted at Lorandir as he dismounted, "Finn the gryphon? Really?"

The elf had the good nature to look embarrassed, "I'm not original when it comes to naming pets, OK."

I snorted with laughter and tried to turn it into a cough as more people stared in my direction. There was no saddle, just a set of leather reigns looping loosely around its beak. I placed my hand cautiously on the soft feathers that covered the gryphon's neck. The creature turned its head to me and nuzzled its beak into my hand. It was beautiful in a fierce sort of way.

Ironfist stepped up, prodding me in the back, "It is a great honour to be escorted by a member of the royal family to the Equinox Ball." He gave a small bow to Lorandir who was looking as discomforted as I had ever seen him. "Allow me to present myself. I am Master Ironfist of the Dwarven Arms Council, escort to Ms Haernson, and it would be an honour to ride with you."

Lorandir looked between the dwarf and me, trying to put two and two together. Schiztz. He thought we were an item. The elf drew himself up and nodded regally at the dwarf, "If you please, it would be my honour to escort Ms Haernson to the palace."

Ironfist nodded and followed Lorandir's gesture to another mount. "Er, I'm not actually your property you know that right?" I grumbled after the dwarf, annoyed that the two men had been discussing me without my involvement.

Lorandir offered me his hand stiffly to help me onto the creature. I whispered to the gryphon, "Don't kill me, OK?" then accepted Lorandir's hand to get onto its back. Its fur was surprisingly comfortable and I settled myself, adjusting my axe and backpack as best I could before gripping onto its feathery neck. It made a noise crossed like a squawk and a roar. The elf swung on behind me. His arms brushed my sides as he reached forward and gripped the reins. "Not too tight," he said softly in my ear.

I nodded and shifted my grip. The gryphon shook its large head and seemed more comfortable. Lorandir dug his knees into Finn's flanks and the gryphon began to move forward at a graceful pace. I felt I had to say something.

"Look, me and Ironfist, I mean, we're not…"

"He's not escorting you to the ball?"

"Well, sort of," I admitted, "but we're not…I mean do you really think…?" I was babbling so decided to be more honest, "It's really good to see you again."

I felt him relax behind me. "It's good to see you again too. I'm glad you accepted the invite."

I tried to twist on the gryphon, "Did you have something to do with that?"

He shrugged and grinned, "It didn't take much to persuade the Council that those who had helped us to return the dragon's egg should be invited to the ball. They're still acting a little oddly, but they're nowhere near as troublesome as they have been."

"Oh, good," I replied stupidly.

It was a longer way than I'd expected to the palace. Groups of less honoured guests moved to one side as we passed. Several bowed. Lorandir shifted uncomfortably each time they did.

I thought back to Ironfist's introduction. "So, are you really royalty?"

"Erm, well, sort of, I guess," he replied sheepishly.

"How can you be sort of royalty?"

He squirmed on the gryphon's back, "I'm sort of nephew to the king…it's not a big thing really, I mean not like my cousin…" He sounded completely embarrassed.

"Dzraking hell," I breathed the curse without thinking.

"Yeah," he agreed.

"So when you said you had to come back to Breconia on family business…"

"My Dad wanted me back here while the dragons were acting strangely, and then there were things to organise with the ball…"

"So, your job is being the king's nephew?" I was genuinely curious. I'd never met a member of a royal family before. In my head I pictured royalty in old fashioned court dresses and fancy outfits and generally unapproachable.

"Sort of, more like general dogsbody when my cousin doesn't feel like doing something. Like organising the ball."

"You've organised the biggest event in the elven calendar?" I was impressed.

I felt him shrug behind me, "Morty – that's my cousin – didn't want to do it and Dad thought it was about time I had some experience in planning royal events. But really, it's not a big deal, there's a lot of precedent to follow."

"Must be a big deal for you though, your first time doing it."

"I'm really nervous actually," he admitted.

I shifted my grip from the gryphon's feathers and squeezed Lorandir's hand, "I'm sure it'll be great."

He leant forward, "I'm glad you're here."

I blushed and tried to lighten the mood, "Well if anything goes wrong, I can always trip over something to be a distraction."

He laughed at that. I was about to tell him it wasn't that funny when we entered an enormous clearing. My breath caught in my throat. The glade was twice, if not three times larger than the clearing the portal had opened onto. A vast tree stood in the centre. Its grey roots were exposed and lifted the trunk at least a storey above the mossy floor. A stream of turquoise water flowed around the palace, forming a moat before disappearing into the forest. Carved roots formed elegant bridges over the water. The tree itself seemed to go on forever, its silvery trunk reaching higher than the rest of the forest canopy. Its canopy was a rich green without a speck of autumn colouring. Twining vines swept delicately around the trunk, creating paths to the upper levels that married nature with architecture.

Lorandir caught my surprise, "Welcome to the Evergreen palace."

We crossed one of the wider roots before the troupe of gryphons stopped outside the palace. Lorandir dismounted confidently before lifting me off. He held me for a moment longer than necessary. My heart skipped as I met his bright green eyes. Then, Finn the gryphon snorted and sidestepped away, ruining the moment. Lorandir released me and I turned away to hide my reddening face.

He turned to face our group and bowed slightly before repeating his words to me more formally for everyone, "Welcome to the Evergreen palace. I will show you to your rooms personally and if you have need of anything, please do not hesitate to ask. The Equinox Ball will begin at six o' clock so until then, feel free to relax in your rooms or, if you wish to see some of the sights of Breconia, I can arrange for a tour."

Aloora lifted her hand, "Where's the library?"

Lorandir smiled, "The palace has a small library, which I'll show you on the way to your suites. The larger Breconian library holds many rare texts and I can ask one of our scholars to escort you to it, if you like."

Aloora nodded eagerly, her eyes shining. I rolled my eyes at her.

With a smile, the elf led the way to one of the vine walkways. It was sturdier and wider than it looked from the ground, but I couldn't see any obvious bannisters to stop people falling. Even Dot seemed a bit apprehensive and she let one of the other elves take the bulky dress bags from her.

I hung back, "Is this the only way up?"

Lorandir thought for a moment, "There is the lift we use to carry provisions to the higher floors, would you prefer to use that?" He indicated a large woven basket attached to a pulley system that was shakily descending from one of the thick branches behind the palace. I watched as elves began loading it with foodstuffs.

I thought briefly of travelling in the swaying lift, but Ironfist answered for me, smiling to cover his own nervousness. "Nonsense, we will travel the same way as the elves," then he hissed to me, "you are representing dwarfdom here, you cannot travel like a sack of potatoes!"

I saw Lorandir cough to cover his laughter. Bloody elven hearing. He pointed to another, slimmer vine snaking around the tree parallel to the steps formed by the larger vines. It was about hand-height for him, or chest height for me. "Please, use this hand rail, or…" he thought for a moment, "…I could have the architects add in guard rails?"

"Nonsense!" replied Ironfist again, "I won't have you spoiling this beautiful palace! We will be quite alright with the handrail, won't we?" He looked pointedly at me, his beard quivering with something between anger and nervousness.

I nodded tightly, "After you." It was cruel, but the dwarf was starting to get on my nerves already.

Dwarf-fully he rose to the challenge and stepped up to the snaking path, taking his place behind Lorandir. Aloora and Dot followed, less apprehensive than me. I swore under my breath and forced myself onto the walkway. Another elf followed me, carrying the dress bags. No help there if I slip and fall, I thought. I gripped the handrail tightly as we made our way up the tree. I forced myself to look at the tree trunk or my hand and tried desperately not to think of the exposed drop to my right. The walkway was formed by many thick vines interwoven together into a sturdy path. The thick stems almost resembled steps, worn smooth by generations of elven feet.

As we ascended, Lorandir played the part of our guide. He stopped briefly at each opening in the thick trunk. I caught the words “library” and “reception hall” but I wasn’t really in the mood for a tour. I just wanted to finish this climb.

As we neared the canopy, the trunk split into several branches, each the width of a small house. He selected one and easily navigated the slight shift in vines to move onto a new pathway. Again, we passed openings in the tree on our way up. Eventually, he turned into a large opening in the silvery branch. We followed him inside to an airy hallway. The walls seemed to glow, creating a shimmering white canvas for the painted frescos. Delicate green leaves adorned the wall, framing painted scenes in green and gold. The paintings flickered softly in the light and I had the strange impression that they were moving slightly.

Lorandir noticed us looking and again played the role of tour guide, “These scenes were painted when this wing was formed. They depict the forming of Breconia and key treaties and alliances formed over the centuries.” He indicated a doorway covered by a huge waxy leaf, “Master Ironfist, I trust this room will be to your satisfaction.” Lorandir slid the leaf to the side and gestured the dwarf inside.

Ironfist looked a little green and I felt a brief pang of sympathy for him as he marched inside, muttering his thanks. Lorandir showed the others to their rooms. Mine was the last one along the corridor, leaving us briefly alone. He looked like he wanted to say something but then the elf carrying the dress bags stepped out of Aloora’s room and joined us in the hall, still carrying my designer bag. Instead,

Lorandir moved the large door leaf to one side and bowed me into my room.

"Thank you…" I stopped. It was easily the most luxurious room I had ever been in. It was dominated by a carved four poster bed, covered with soft linens embroidered with three-lobed leaves that might have been ivy. The floor was covered with woven matting that was soft and springy underfoot.

"I hope you like your room," Lorandir interrupted my awe of the interior. The serving elf hastily entered and hung up the dress bag in an alcove set into the wall of the room before bowing and exiting. Lorandir seemed a little nervous, "I'll leave you to unpack. Erm, if you have time, I'd love to show you around, I mean…if you want to…"

I placed my hand on his, "I'd love that."

His face broke into a grin. I'd forgotten how handsome he was when he smiled. He twisted his grip and lifted my hand to his mouth. He bowed over it slightly then pressed his lips to the back of my hand. It was the most romantic gesture I'd ever experienced. My breath caught in my chest. My heart skipped a beat. "I'll find you in an hour." He kissed my hand again and then left, pushing the door leaf into place as if it were a sliding door.

Wow. My head was reeling as I gazed around the room again, trying to enjoy my surroundings and process what was happening in my heart. I decided to explore the suite first and deal with my feelings later. There were two more waxy leaf doorways that led off the bedroom. I slid the first one across and gasped. It was the most beautiful bathroom I had ever seen.

There was a deep bathtub carved from light-coloured wood under silvery wooden taps. Bottles of scented products lined the side of the tub. I sniffed one and the scent of fresh cut meadow flowers made my head spin. The large sink was also carved from wood with more wooden taps and even the toilet was wooden. I guessed the stereotypes about elves being really into nature was true. Small starry lights illuminated a mirror set into an elegant wooden frame and provided flattering lighting. I smiled. I would definitely have to try that bath out before I left.

Humming happily, I walked past a small window with some gauzy material tied to form a curtain and tried the second door leaf off the bedroom. I froze. This opening led onto a balcony and I realised just how high up in the canopy we were. Fortunately there was a balustrade, again, formed from intertwining vines, but all I could see were the tops of trees. I forced myself to go and look. I edged my way along the wall to the bannister. I gripped the vines tightly and peeked over. Instantly I felt my head swim and my stomach sink. We were above the forest canopy and the ground was a long, long way down. I forced myself to take a deep breath and step back inside. Needless to say I would not be venturing out there again. Once in the safety of the bedroom, I gulped air back into my lungs. I realised I was shaking and decided to lie down. The bed was soft and comfortable. The clean linen sheets were the highest thread count I had ever felt. I moaned aloud and allowed my eyes to close as I enjoyed the pleasure of crisp bedding.

I woke with a start. It took me a couple of minutes to get my bearings. Then I stretched and grabbed my phone.

Schiztz! I'd been asleep for fifty minutes. And Lorandir was coming back in ten minutes! I called Aloora desperately.

She answered immediately and very excitedly, "OMG did you see the bath!"

"Yeah, the bath's great, I can't wait to try it…"

"You haven't tried it yet?! What have you been doing for the last hour?!"

"I've been in bed."

"Isn't it gorgeously soft? Wait a minute, did you hook up with the elf?! I knew it! Tell me everything!"

"Woah, slow down. I've been sleeping on the bed!" I felt myself blushing even though there was no one else in the room with me.

"Boring."

"And Lorandir's going to be here in eight minutes. What do I do?"

"I knew it! What do you mean 'what do you do'? Just answer the door wearing nothing but a smile and try to keep it down. I'm in the room next to you, you know."

"Ally! Please, I need help. What should I wear?"

"What did you bring with you?"

I thought a moment, "Just jeans and a spare t-shirt. Schiztz this is bad."

"No, it's fine, it's casual and he likes you anyway. Just put on a bit of make-up, do something with your hair and wear some good underwear. Now go, shoo, get ready and give me all the details later." She hung up.

Now I was more nervous than before. I didn't even have any good underwear, just the cotton pants I had bought during the week. I raced into the bathroom and glared at the mirror. I debated changing my clothes but decided that the jeans hugged my curves nicely and the t-shirt would make it look like I wasn't trying too hard. I hastily swept some mascara over my eyelashes and some tinted lip balm onto my lips. It would have to do. My hair was super frizzy after my nap and I tugged a hairbrush through it savagely, trying to tame it into submission. It remained stubbornly untidy so I plaited it into two braids in record time, swearing as one elastic hairband pinged from my hand onto the floor. I bent to retrieve it and as I stood, I cracked my head on the side of the wooden sink.

"Dzrak! Dzrak dzrakity dzrak balls!" I swore as I finished the plait and then rubbed my head, instantly re-frizzing my hair. I cursed again and frantically tried to flatten it down with water. This was not going well. I heard a light knock on wood. Schiztz, he was here. I forced myself to take three deep breaths with my eyes closed, one hand wrapped around my amethyst necklace to ground myself. Then I looked myself in the eye, "Get it together Ame!" I scolded myself. Shoving my phone into my pocket, I slid the leaf out from the opening like a Japanese screen door.

"Hi," I unintentionally sounded breathy. Dzrak it.

"Hi," Lorandir sounded a little nervous too, "how was your room?"

"It's really great. I love the bed, I've never slept in a four poster before." Now I was rambling. What an idiot.

His eyes flicked from me to the bed and back again with a small smile now playing on his lips. The elf had the uncanny ability to go from tense to arrogantly flirtatious in an instant. Annoyed with myself for drawing his attention to the bed, I stepped into the hallway and slid the leaf door shut, blocking the view into my room.

"So, what did you have planned?"

He raised an eyebrow playfully and I felt my cheeks heat. I dug my nails into the palms of my hands in an effort to distract myself. "I thought you might like to see some of the sights of Breconia before the ball later, if you would allow me to accompany you." He gave a small bow.

"Lead on," I replied stupidly.

"If you don't mind, I did promise to show Aloora the library…"

"Of course," I felt a small pang of jealousy that he was thinking of my friend. I was a complete idiot. Maybe he was just being polite after all and I was misreading things. He moved to her room and knocked on the wood to one side of the large green leaf. Aloora poked her head out and her eyes widened. She looked between us in confusion.

Lorandir coughed awkwardly, "You said you were interested in seeing the library?"

"Oh, right, yes. Of course. I'll just get dressed."

I gave her a look of disbelief. She caught my eye, "What? The bath was a-ma-zing!" She scurried back into her room, leaving me and Lorandir making awkward small talk in the hallway. For something to say, he began explaining a nearby painting to me. I feigned interest in the depiction of some ancient elven King forging an alliance with the dwarves and the fae to go to war with the Mostrim. I pushed to the back of my mind the disturbing notion of one of the Mostrim being after me, after all they were extinct and I wasn't sure I trusted the kobold who'd gleefully given me the information.

Partway through the description, Ironfist joined us in the hall. Unlike me, he seemed genuinely interested and plied Lorandir with detailed questions about the artist and subjects.

Aloora stepped outside as we entered an awkward silence. She looked between us and this time shook her head at me.

"Lead on," she gestured to the elf.

"Oh, where are you going? I wonder if I might join you?" Ironfist fell into step behind us.

"Er, we're taking Aloora to the library and then Lorandir's showing me around," I replied.

"Excellent! I'd love to see the city. Lead on!"

Schiztz. The last thing I wanted was for Ironfist to be part of our date, or whatever it was. I was starting to like the elf.

Lorandir paused at the start of the vine staircase, "Of course, Master Ironfist. I know our prince was keen to meet with you as well, you must allow me to introduce you."

The dwarf puffed out his chest in pride and nodded courteously.

"Then let us descend," Lorandir continued as he stepped lightly onto the vines.

I paused and asked hopefully, "Is this the only way to get down?"

The elf tilted his head to one side, considering, "I could call up the gryphons..."

"No, no, it's fine. I'll walk." I started to feel nauseous just thinking about flying down on the gryphons.

The descent seemed to go faster than the journey to our rooms. The vine walkways spiralled around the vast tree trunk in the opposite direction to the one we had ascended, meaning we wouldn't have to navigate anyone trying to come up on the narrow path. I concentrated on watching my feet and holding tightly to the handrail. I could hear Ironfist muttering behind me on the way down. It helped take my mind off the long fall to my left and I learned some valuable new Dwarfish curse words. I stored up 'cocht-wimble' for later.

Partway down, Lorandir paused at a large entrance in the trunk and turned easily. "This is the library, I have arranged for one of our scholars to give you a tour of some of our more valuable and rare tomes here. If you would also like to see the larger Breconian library, Shesalva will be more than happy to accompany you." As he spoke her name, a tall beautiful elf with red hair appeared at the entrance and held out her hand. Aloora took it gently and said something in Elvish. Shesalva nodded and smiled. They disappeared into the library together.

"See you later," I called after my friend. I got a vague wave in return as she disappeared among the shelves.

Lorandir gestured to the walkway, "Shall we continue?"

I swallowed and nodded. He gave me a small wink and carried on at a slow pace so me and Ironfist could keep up. After a shorter time than I was expecting, we stepped onto the mossy forest floor in the clearing around the palace tree. I resisted the urge to hug the floor, but it was a close call.

Ironfist seemed happier on the ground too, "Where to now then?" He rubbed his hands together in anticipation.

Lorandir walked towards the exposed roots that formed the ground floor of the palace, "This is the ballroom where the Equinox Ball will take place tonight. Usually it is more of a court room where the Council meetings are held and the King holds court. We are in the process of transforming it for tonight's entertainment."

He led us between two intertwined roots into the space. Inside, the roots were painted with gold. Elves hurried around setting up tables and hanging expensive looking tapestries around the space. I saw two elves arguing passionately as they changed glowing orbs from green to yellow. Lorandir rushed over, "Soft candlelight please, no effects."

Chastened, the elves bowed and immediately dimmed the orbs to a more sedate yellow glow that mimicked soft candlelight.

Ironfist was looking round, taking everything in and uttering compliments about everything he could see. Lorandir's smile was beginning to seem tense. I ignored them both and wondered how the room stayed dry when it rained with all the open sides. My unspoken question was answered when a female elf dressed in blue began wielding her magic around the tree roots. Green magic spun from her hands and the roots seemed to grow, intertwine and shrink at her command. Soon, an entire section of the room now had an elegant wall. With another flick of her hands, the interior became the same shade of gold as the rest of the room. I realised my mouth was hanging open and shut it quickly.

"Ah, Master Ironfist," Lorandir interrupted the flow of compliments, "allow me to introduce Prince Morthimas. Morty, this is the dwarven representative I was telling you about."

A tall elf with long blonde hair and similar colouring to Lorandir strode over and smiled. Ironfist bowed. I wondered if I should curtsy, but I didn't know how so I copied the dwarf's lead and bowed slightly.

"And the lovely Amethyst, I see. Now you, I have heard much about." The Prince's eyes looked me up and down with a trace of humour in them.

I crossed my arms, "Oh really?" I wasn't about to be laughed at by an elf, even if he was royal.

Lorandir stepped in smoothly, "Master Ironfist is keen to have a tour of Breconia, I can think of no one better to show him around than you cousin."

The Prince quirked an eyebrow at Lorandir. There was some unspoken conversation going on between them. Then Morty smiled, "Of course, if you please Master Ironfist, allow me to show you the sights of Breconia. I normally start these tours with the state rooms…" He led the dwarf away through another passage between the roots.

"What was that about?" I demanded.

"Hmm? Oh, well Morty will keep your chaperone busy so we can explore."

“No. What did he mean about hearing so much about me?”

Lorandir took my arm and tucked it into the crook of his before steering me out of the main hall, “Nothing. My cousin likes to make trouble that’s all. Now, I’ve got a surprise for you.”

I didn’t know what to say to that. I was relieved that it was just a joke, although I needed to readjust my sense of humour before I offended more royalty. In the back of my mind, I was also sort of disappointed that Lorandir hadn’t mentioned me to his friends.

Chapter 18

Lorandir led me around the clearing over a bridge made from the pale silvery roots of the palace tree. It was exquisite craftsmanship. The roots twined around one another to form a wide path over the turquoise water that glistened in the sun. It really was a beautiful place.

"Where are we going?" I asked curiously as I looked around, trying to take everything in.

Lorandir looked at me with a cheeky grin on his face, but shook his head. Fine, a surprise it would be. He walked us away from the palace tree along a narrow pathway of springy moss. The trees gave just the right amount of shade and dappled light hit the forest floor in hazy patterns.

"Did the forest grow like this naturally?" I asked in wonder as we passed trees that seemed to compliment each other so well.

The elf shook his head, "Not exactly. The forest has been carefully curated to ensure the trees have the right amount of light and space. Our architects work on selecting the best trees for housing as well and cultivate them from an early age." He pointed to a young sapling with a blue piece of fabric tied to it. I could feel strong magic coming from it over the innate elven magic that permeated the air in Breconia.

"That's a ward," Lorandir answered my unspoken question, "it makes sure no animals eat or trample the trees before they can take care of themselves."

A vision flashed into my eyes of a tree whipping its branches around to defend itself from a deer. "Trees can't really defend themselves can they?"

"Well I wouldn't like to mess with some of the more ancient trees here," he grinned.

"There aren't many houses here," I observed as the sounds of people preparing for the party of the year faded from hearing. The forest was now tranquil and I could clearly hear birdsong as the small creatures flitted among the branches.

Lorandir nodded, "This is the outskirts of the city. We'll soon be in the nature reserve itself." He continued on confidently.

A rustle sounded from the side of the path. Suddenly the tranquil forest seemed a lot more menacing. There was less sunlight here and less noise. The forest floor was less well-maintained and bushes and shrubs grew alongside ferns in the shade of the wilder canopies. A horrible thought crossed my mind: tarfangtulas lived in the Breconian forest. And I had left my axe in my room. And we were now so deep in the forests, would anyone even hear if I screamed. I had to ask, "Erm, the tarfangtulas…"

Lorandir shook his head, “They stay far away from the city. It’s very unusual to see them.”

I thought about my two previous encounters with the ten-legged spider monsters. Then what he’d said registered in my mind. ‘Unusual to see them’ wasn’t actually that comforting. As those thoughts played in my head, something moved in the undergrowth. I stopped and gripped his arm. Panic rose in my chest. My heart pounded as adrenaline began to pump through me. More rustling. The bushes parted. A small deer scurried across the path. I sighed in relief.

The elf seemed to be thinking, “It would be more likely we’d see a chimera this close to the city.”

I froze. A chimera?! A fire-breathing snake-lion-dragon?! I’d only seen pictures of them and had no desire to see one up close. I looked behind me, wondering if we should go back. He patted me on the arm, “Hey, I’m just kidding.”

“Of course,” I was definitely out of my element here.

We kept going. He pointed out various interesting plants, some were laden with ripe berries and others were just green leaves. I pretended to listen whilst keeping my senses sharp for approaching monsters. After a little way, he turned off the path into the dark forest itself. It was too narrow for us to walk side by side so he led the way, holding ferns and brambles to one side like a gentleman when they crossed over our path. Bright fluted flowers provided a burst of colour in the middle of all the different browns and greens.

“I’m surprised you elves let brambles grow in your forest,” I complained as one snagged my jeans.

“Where else will we get blackberries from?” he grinned as he popped a plump berry in his mouth. He looked so adorable eating foraged berries that I grinned back and helped myself to a blackberry. It was perfectly ripe and burst in my mouth in a riot of sweetness.

“Nothing beats fresh fruit,” he smiled and bowed me forward. I snagged another berry realising I was hungry.

“So where are we going?” I asked again. My legs were tired after climbing up and down that tree and now walking into a forest.

“We’re nearly there. Just past those trees,” he pointed. I thought I saw a patch of light shining between two of the large pine trees in front of us. I followed the elf, letting him pick the best path through the ferns. I must not have followed him exactly as I managed to get caught in some trailing vines. I pulled at them, trying to free myself and managed to stumble forward between the trees. I was brushing sticky bits of plant off me when I looked up. I stopped.

It was breathtakingly beautiful. We were in a clearing on top of a small rise. The forest swept down in front of us in swathes of greens, yellows and reds. In the distance were the tall mountains that sheltered the dragons. In the afternoon sun, the mountains were a lush, fertile green. Everything looked more intense that I had ever seen before. A small rocky outcrop sat in the centre of the clearing and below it swirled a pool of turquoise water.

“It’s beautiful,” I breathed.

Lorandir smiled at me, “This is my favourite spot in all Breconia. I used to come here when I wanted to get away from everything and sit on that rock and just stare at it all. I could lose myself here for hours."

He led me up to the rock, then climbed it easily. He offered me his hand. I took it and scrambled up behind him. He sat at the top and pulled me down next to him. The stone was warm beneath my jeans. I gazed out at the view. I could see why it was one of his favourite spots.

Lorandir brought me out of my reverie by unpacking a small satchel I hadn't noticed he was wearing. He handed me a packet made of a beeswax wrap.

"What is it?" I started unwrapping it.

"I thought you might be hungry," he replied, unpacking his own wrap. Guess he knew me well. I finished removing the waxy material to expose a triangle of buttery pastry. This was looking promising. I sniffed it before taking a large bite. The pastry melted in my mouth and then, a second later, the filling hit my taste buds. I tasted a mixture of cheese and greens. It was pretty good, but I wasn't converted to vegetarianism.

"Nice," I told him between mouthfuls. I didn't want to seem greedy, but the small pastry had done nothing to fill my stomach.

"The best is yet to come. Try this," he seemed to be amused as he passed me another parcel, about the same size.

I unwrapped it carefully, not enjoying being the source of amusement. This one was softer and as I opened the material, I was disappointed to see green leaves. "What is it?" I tried to keep the disdain out of my voice.

He laughed, "Try it, you'll like it." I was still reluctant to bite into something so obviously healthy, but I decided to give it a go. The worst it could be was bland.

I nibbled one corner. The leaves were surprisingly sweet and the filling inside filled my mouth with creamy, rich chocolate and a hint of hazelnut. It was delicious. "This is really good!" I was surprised and finished it with relish.

"Told you," he handed me another and we ate in companionable silence.

We quickly demolished all the food Lorandir had thoughtfully brought with us and sat enjoying the scenery. As I relaxed, I sat back, placing my hands behind me on the rough surface of the rock to take my weigh. I wasn't expecting to feel anything in the stone, but a tell-tale jewel called to my crafting senses.

"It's a quartz geode!" I exclaimed.

He gave me a look, "I wondered if you'd notice." He led me down from our seat and around the other side to the pool of water. From this side, I could see that the geode had split, exposing the quartz crystals inside. The water reflected the shiny jewels and the crystals reflected the light creating a dazzling display of shimmering colours. I knelt down and trailed my fingers in the pool, tracing one of the rainbows created by the refraction. I was expecting the water to be cold, but it was the perfect bathing temperature.

"A hot spring!" This place was full of surprises. I calmed myself down. It was only a bit of water. "So what now?"

"We could go swimming," the elf suggested.

I frowned, "I haven't brought a costume."

"Neither have I." He pulled his shirt over his head. I felt the blush starting to heat my face. I opened and closed my mouth stupidly as I tried to think of a good response whilst avoiding staring at his muscled chest. I was saved from having to reply by a loud rustle in the forest. I turned quickly, grateful for the distraction.

"What was that?"

"Nothing, just some animal…"

Said animal came crashing into the clearing. It stopped as it saw us, opened one of its fanged mouths and roared. The force of it made me step back. My brain was trying to process what my eyes were seeing. My body had more sense and scrabbled up the rock, backing away. Lorandir had the same idea.

"Just stay still and calm," he hissed at me, "it'll see we're not a threat and go away."

I nodded blankly while watching its two heads. The chimera seemed to have one pair of eyes trained on each of us. Both of them roared this time. I was expecting it from the large lion's head, but the sound of a feral goat roaring was truly hideous. A combination of a bleat and someone coughing up phlegm. I wasn't as optimistic as Lorandir and guessed the reason it hadn't attacked yet was because it hadn't decided which one of us to kill first. I silently cursed that I hadn't brought my axe with me and made a mental note that, if I survived, I would never leave it behind again. I did a quick inventory. I had my fire charm earrings in, my amethyst necklace that was meant to give me protection, but I had no idea how that worked. It didn't seem a great idea to risk my life trying to find out. My keyring had the charm that allowed me to see through elven glamour, although it didn't seem to be protecting me from Lorandir's charms. The only protective clothing I was wearing were my thick gothic-style leather boots. I didn't really want to test them against the chimera's teeth either. Schiztz. I expanded my inventory to include Lorandir. He wasn't carrying his sword but he had magic, surely he could do something.

While I was thinking, the elf must have had a similar idea. He loosed off a bolt of magic which caused a branch from a nearby tree to fall. The chimera turned, distracted. We used that moment to leap from the rock to the ground. I landed hard but pushed myself up and ran to the tree line away from the monster. With a pee-inducing scream, the chimera realised we were getting away and bounded after us. Lorandir was already at the trees. Bloody elven agility. I felt a blast of heat behind me and risked looking over my shoulder. The creature was breathing fire from both its mouths. Looks like my fire charm was going to come in useful after all! I weaved to one side, trying to confuse it. It didn't work. With a leap, it was on me. I felt its heavy weight as it pushed me to the ground. I heard another blast of magic from the trees and an ear-splitting roar. The pressure lifted from my back. Instinctively, I rolled onto my back so I was now facing it. But I was still on the ground. Four eyes were looking at Lorandir, who was throwing bolts of energy at it. That just seemed to be pissing it off. I wriggled backwards in a strange crab shuffle. A snake's head appeared in my vision. Schiztz. Where had that come from?!

The snake bared its fangs with a hiss and struck down at me. I shifted to one side with a speed I hadn't known I possessed. I sent a silent thank you to Espretha for her training. The fangs pierced my t-shirt. Too close for my liking. I tried to get away. The chimera twisted itself round. I was dragged with it. The snake's head was still stuck in my top. I scrabbled for purchase as the snake reared up, back into its tail position. My feet were soon dangling over mid-air. I kicked wildly and my boots connected with something soft. Its family jewels. The chimera gave a high pitched squeal and tried to turn to get me. I was whirled round with it as it tried to chase its own tail to bite me. A blast of magic singed past my ear.

"You're going to hit me!" I shouted at Lorandir as I flailed my arms wildly. I managed to grab onto the snake's neck behind its head. Or should that be chimera's tail? I was dizzy and disorientated. I heard a high-pitched whistle. I wondered briefly if my brain was affected by the spinning. The creature was still running in circles, two jaws snapping furiously at my heels. The snake managed to shake itself free from my t-shirt. It hissed and coiled in my grasp. Dzrak. I shifted my grip and swung down. Both boots connected hard with its special area. The monster let out something between a gasp and a guttural groan. Even the snake managed to groan. It fell to its knees. I released the tail and ran. It staggered upwards, eyes full of hatred as it stumbled after me. I plunged into the forest. Lorandir was beside me and looking upwards.

I didn't have the breath to ask why he wasn't looking at the murderous monster heading for us. I glanced back over my shoulder. And tripped over an exposed tree root. I sprawled headlong into a bramble bush. “Arg!” I cried out as the thorns pricked into me.

I felt teeth clamp down on one of my boots. Dzrak. I was pulled painfully out of the bush. This was it. I wasn’t going down without a fight. I tried to twist and kick with my free foot. I hit the chimera in one of its mouths. It dropped me and stood over me. I saw a flicker of light in its throat and closed my eyes against the fire forming in its maw. Saliva dripped onto me. I heard another roar. I braced myself for the heat. Then a hiss of pain sounded. No fire. I wasn’t dead! I opened my eyes cautiously. Finn, the gryphon, stood over the bloodied body of the chimera. He clawed at it with his talons as it thrashed beneath him. The gryphon looked proud of himself and pecked at it with his beak, tearing off chunks of flesh and gulping them down.

“Good job, boy,” I managed weakly. Lorandir offered his hand then hoisted me to my feet. He was unscathed and fully dressed. He always seemed to come out of these fights better than me.

Finn stepped away from the remains of the creature and nuzzled me, covering me with the blood from his beak. I stroked his feathery neck gratefully. The gryphon knelt its front legs down so I could mount it and I straddled it gingerly. I wasn’t sure I trusted myself to walk back. My hands were shaking from the adrenaline of fighting a mythical monster. Lorandir slid into place behind me on the creature’s broad back. With a kick of his heels, we were airborne.

“Oh…dzrak…” I called as the gryphon rocketed upwards through the canopy. I held on tightly, my head buried in his soft neck as we flew back towards the palace clearing.

Chapter 19

Finn landed gently in the clearing. Elves bustled around us as I slipped down and resisted the urge to hug the mossy floor. Lorandir was talking in rapid Elvish to one of the guards and gesturing to the forest. I heard something that sounded like "chimera" and guessed he was reporting the attack. Someone led Finn away to the stables, or whatever the equivalent is for gryphons. I pulled out my phone, to distract myself from my churning stomach and noticed the time. Only two hours until the ball started. Normally I'd be ready for a night out in fifteen minutes flat but I had a feeling that unless I made a proper effort with my hair and make-up, Ironfist would insist on doing it himself.

Lorandir stepped to my side. "Are you alright?" he asked taking in the scratches on my arms.

"Don't even worry about it, I'm fine," I brushed off his concern, "not looking forward to climbing those vines again." I looked up and gave an exaggerated shudder to lighten the mood.

He looked thoughtful, “The portals should be ready by now…” He tucked my arm into his and led us to an entranceway to the ballroom. There were a lot fewer ways in than when we had left. Those architects had been busy. He gestured towards a row of shimmering portals. “The one at the far end leads to your floor.”

I stared at him, “Are you telling me there’s a way to get down from my room without using the death walk?!”

He shifted his feet, “They’ve been set up for the ball.”

Realising I was being less than grateful, I patted his hand, “Thank you, and thank you for showing me the clearing. It was beautiful. You know, until we got attacked by a monster.” On impulse, I stood on tiptoes and kissed his cheek before walking quickly through the portal. I looked back as I stepped through and saw him touching his cheek and grinning at me before he was accosted by an elf with a leaf clipboard.

With a sucking, rushing sensation and a swirl of forest leaves, I found myself in the corridor where our bedrooms were. I began walking to my room and had just passed Aloora’s leaf door when I heard her push it aside.

“I thought I heard a portal,” she reached up and plucked something from my hair, “I see you had a good time!”

I turned to face her. She was twirling a small leaf between her fingers and smiling knowingly at me. Her face changed as she took in the tear in my t-shirt and the grazes on my arms.

“A chimera attacked us,” I shrugged it off as if it was something normal, “how was the library?”

"Holy hand grenades, are you OK?"

"Don't even worry about it. Since when did you start watching Monty Python?"

It was her turn to shrug, "Dot's really into it, and it's not all busy, busy at the Office." She gave me an appraising look, "Bath, then I'll come over to help with your hair and make-up."

I gave her an impromptu hug, "You're a good friend."

"I know, now go get washed."

I was happy to slide the large leaf behind me as I entered my room. It had been a weird day, and now I had to get ready to go to a fancy ball. I had never really expected anything like this to happen. I took a deep breath and thought through what I had to do for the rest of the evening: bath, get dressed, let Aloora do her best with my unruly hair and chubby face, call Uncle Owain for my daily Errol update, and, most importantly, go to the ball and try not to embarrass myself.

I wondered about adding a sixth item to my mental list involving a handsome, if arrogant, elf, but I decided to worry about that later.

With that decision made, I headed for the bathroom. The plug was a simple wooden cork and I wedged it into the plughole before turning on the wooden tap. Steaming hot turquoise water instantly began filling up the polished wooden tub. I added some fragrant liquid which I guessed was bubble bath to the water and it started frothing into foamy bubbles with the smell of meadow flowers. It filled up quickly and I sank gratefully into the bubbles. I exhaled as I let the hot water surround me and felt some of the tension I was carrying in my shoulders begin to ease. The elves definitely had it good when it came to bathing. As I relaxed, I wondered why the water was such a vibrant colour. My magic began to tingle and I felt the minute particles of copper and other minerals within the water. Not so much of a mystery after all. My thoughts began to drift to the pool filled with the same water earlier today and the half-naked elf standing next to it…

When my fingers had turned wrinkly, I decided it was time to shave my legs and get out. I heard my phone ping in the bedroom as a text message arrived and decided to ignore it. I grabbed a fluffy white towel from a shelf and wrapped myself in it before letting the now lukewarm water out of the bath. I hoped there was time to enjoy that experience again tomorrow morning before we left.

I dried myself without even bothering to glance in the steamed up mirror and then spotted the silky green robe hanging from a carved hook. I pulled it on, enjoying the way the fabric moved against my skin. I felt like some sort of glamourous screen goddess from the days of black and white cinema. Smiling to myself, I headed back into the bedroom. I froze. Standing there was a gorgeous female elf with blonde hair falling to her waist.

"Please," she gestured with one slender arm to a table now set up in my room.

"Er, I think you've got the wrong room," I said stupidly.

She shook her head with a slow smile, "As an honoured guest, I am here to help with your preparations for tonight." Her voice was accented slightly, but it still sounded like verbal honey. Belatedly, I remembered my anti-glamour charm was still in my jeans.

"Just let me…" I grabbed my phone to text Aloora for help. I saw a message from her:

There's an elf in your room. Go with it. See you soon x

OK, I guessed I'd go with it then. I looked at the elf again. She didn't seem like a threat in her long flowing robes. I was starting to get paranoid.

"What's the plan?" I asked the elf lady.

She smiled again, "We will start with a massage." She gestured to the table and I lay on it tensely, face down with my head supported in a cut out for my face.

She rolled my robe down off the upper half of my body and began kneading me with expert hands covered in fragrant oil. I felt all the tension leave my muscles as she worked. Then her magic began to flow into me, healing the grazes on my arm and releasing deep-seated tension I didn't even know I was carrying. I briefly thought it was odd that her magic felt different to Lorandir's healing magic. I'd expected all elven magic to feel the same, but his was bittersweet chocolate, honey mead and leafy forests whereas hers felt more like freshly mown grass and lavender. Then all thoughts left my head as I relaxed under her hands.

She stopped and let me lie there for a few minutes to come back to reality. I pushed myself up in a daze and realised I'd been drooling on the table. The elf had backed off and was modestly facing the window. I covered myself hastily with my robe and wiped at the saliva ineffectually with a sleeve. I succeeded in smearing it around into a thin layer. That would have to do.

"And now for hair," the elf turned and with another smile gestured to a stool I hadn't noticed before in front of a full length mirror. "Did you have any thoughts on how you wanted to wear it?"

"Erm no," I replied honestly. I had intended to leave that to Aloora and my expectations were pretty low. My hair was thick and frizzy, normally the best I could do was plait it and hope.

The elf tilted her head from side to side as she assessed my hair, still damp from the bath. She ran her hands over it and, with a crackle of magic, it dried instantly into a tangle of frizz. I plucked at it apologetically. She tapped a long finger to the side of her face thoughtfully, deciding how best to approach this challenge. She made a decision and rummaged through an elegant wooden box decorated with etchings on leaves and squirted some liquid onto her hands. As she smoothed it through my hair, I was amazed to see the flyaway hairs disappearing and soon my locks were smooth and full.

"Wow," I looked at myself in the mirror, turning my head to admire my glossy hair. Without the frizz, it had a deeper reddish tint to it and was longer than I had realised. "What is that stuff?"

"It is a special elven conditioner of my own design, would you like me to leave you a bottle?"

I nodded eagerly. That stuff was amazing. She smiled again and this time it seemed more genuine than before. She ran a brush through my hair in long, slow strokes. It felt divine. I was enjoying the pampering when she stopped and began yanking my hair back into a complicated plait. I winced and tried to keep still as any time I moved, she pulled harder.

"There," she took a small step back and admired her work. I stared at myself in the mirror. The elf had outdone herself. My usually unruly mane had been tamed into an elegant half up, half down hair do.

"Thank you," I gushed. I hadn't realised I could look sophisticated.

Aloora burst into the room, sliding the leaf to one side with a flourish. She was already dressed and ready. Her midnight blue dress hung perfectly on her petite frame, a subtle split up one side made her legs look long and lean. She was balanced on golden shoes with a heel shaped like a dragon's tail and carrying two bags. One was an elegant midnight blue and gold construction and the other was her familiar over-stuffed make-up bag. Another elf dressed in the same flowing robes as my attendant swept in behind her.

"Wow!" I exclaimed, standing up, "You look amazing!"

"As do you! I never knew your hair could look like that."

I patted it gently, earning a furrowed brow from the elf. I put my hand down like a naughty school girl.

"Have you seen your dress yet? What make-up are you going for?"

"No and no idea," I had honestly forgotten to look at my outfit for tonight. Aloora grabbed my hand enthusiastically and pulled me towards the alcove where the designer bag hung.

"Well, go on then!"

With some trepidation, I unzipped the bag. Swathes of deep burgundy material greeted me. I struggled with the bag and the hanger until finally it was free. It looked rich and gorgeous with a corset style top and a fitted skirt. It also had a slit cut into it. Aloora gushed over the dress, praising the details and fabric. I stood mute. Schiztz. How was I going to pull off an outfit like this? I was used to jeans and maybe some steampunk style corsets but this was another level.

Aloora had dug out a small fabric bag and was delicately lifting out some underwear. Thank goodness! I had only packed plain pants and bras, not the support system I'd need to fit into this creation. My friend found another bag containing shoes. I was relieved to see they weren't as high as her own daggers, but they looked feminine and a far cry from my heavy duty boots.

"With your natural colouring and this gorgeous dress, I'd suggest keeping the make-up subtle and focusing on the eyes," the elf interrupted my internal monologue. I nodded along as if I had a clue what she was talking about.

My friend was more enthusiastic, "I agree, maybe some copper highlights to go with the necklace. Are you wearing your amethyst pendent?"

"Yes, yes," I was being swept along in their flow. "Wait! I have something for you, before I forget." I dug through my backpack, abandoned on the floor until I found the collar I had created for my friend. I took it out and handed it to her.

The large dragon scale caught the light delicately. I had set it into a thick gold collar, beaten with a small hammer for a weathered, more ancient feel. It was the finest piece I had ever created. She gazed at it reverently.

"This is for me?" she squeaked. I nodded. "But it's got your dragon scale in it!" She ran her slim fingers over the scale.

I nodded again, smiling at her excitement, "I thought you'd appreciate it more than me. Do you like it?" I was suddenly anxious about my creation.

She looked at me with tears in her eyes, "It's gorgeous. Thank you!" She flung her arms around me in a hug and squeezed tightly. "Will you put it on for me?"

I smiled and took the necklace from her, placing it round her neck and doing up the clasp. I was pleased to see that it fit perfectly and complemented her dress well. She admired herself in the mirror and removed the chunky cocktail ring she had on her right ring finger. "I don't want anything to distract from this!"

In a buzz of happiness at her reaction to my gift, I allowed the two elves and my friend to fuss with my face as they applied foundation, eyeshadow, mascara and lipstick. When they were finished, I looked at the mirror and almost didn't recognise myself. My normally dull brown eyes sparkled and looked huge, my skin was flawless and my lips were luscious. "Is it magic?" I whispered as I moved my hand to touch my face then stopped as I didn't want to ruin anything.

The elves laughed, "Just make-up to enhance your natural beauty."

I pulled a face; that seemed unlikely. I was convinced they'd done something. Then I remembered to be polite, "Thank you." It seemed too little but they smiled back at me and packed up their things into the slim wooden box before leaving Aloora and I alone together.

"Let's get you dressed before Ironfist bursts in!" she giggled.

I rolled my eyes, "Don't even joke!" I hurried over to the dress bag and struggled into the underwear before pulling on the dress. I zipped it up on the side and turned to the mirror. Dzraking hell! I looked amazing! It fit like a dream and somehow Madame Tinselle's creation had enhanced my curves in just the right way. I had no idea how it was staying up without straps but it looked good. I slipped on my shoes and completed the illusion. I looked like someone going to a fancy ball.

Just in time. A sharp knock came from the doorway. I shouted "Come in!"

When Ironfist strode through the door with Dot in tow, I was still staring at the mirror in disbelief at my transformation.

Dot gave a low whistle, "Very nice both of you. Did you have an elf help you too?"

I nodded while Aloora preened herself and pointed her toes to show off her shoes. Dot was in a straight black gown fit for a supermodel. It suited her really well and I complimented her on the vintage look.

She laughed, "Vintage? This is an original Chanel! There are some perks to living so long!"

Ironfist was giving me a more professional look whilst picking a non-existent piece of lint from his kilt, "Yes, you'll make a good representative for dwarfdom."

"That was almost a compliment! Careful or I'll think you're going soft."

He furrowed his brow. Oops. Probably not a great idea to annoy the person who had paid for my outfit. "I mean, er, thank you for getting Madame to do this. The dresses are gorgeous."

He nodded regally then pulled out a golden pocket watch, "We should go, I don't want to be late."

"Hang on, I just need to say goodnight to Errol," I disappeared into the bathroom with my phone to call Uncle Owain. He insisted on showing me Errol's neighbours as well as my own wyrm. I was pleased to see he was doing well but it was hard not having him with me; he was my closest friend and constant companion. Before I hung up, he did a little somersault and nearly set my Uncle's hair on fire. Typical Errol. I smiled to myself before leaving the bathroom.

Back in the bedroom, Ironfist was tapping his foot and Dot and Aloora were snapping pictures of each other. I had questions about whether Dot would show up in them, weren't vampires not meant to have reflections? Did that count for cameras too? But Ironfist was standing by the door and gesturing. I was worried about a vein that had appeared in his forehead.

We started to walk out of the room. I grabbed my axe and everyone turned to look at me. "What?!"

“I don’t think you’ll need that at a ball,” Dot was looking perplexed.

“Yeah, well, I didn’t think I’d need it for a stroll in the woods but there are chimeras out there, and tarfangtulas and dzrak knows what else.” I looked to Ironfist for support as he had a smaller traditional pickaxe attached to a low slung belt and I suspected there was at least one knife in his sporran. “Isn’t it a cultural thing to represent my dwarfishness?”

I could see the struggle behind his beard. On the one hand, my axe wasn’t exactly evening wear. On the other, it was definitely dwarven. “Yes, yes it is a good symbol to show you’re proud of your heritage.” I stopped myself doing a fist pump and instead hefted Bane over my shoulder. “However, you cannot wear it like that. Allow me.”

He moved his hands over the elegant copper chain on the evening bag that Madam had designed. Somehow he created loops to hold the axe securely and I could close the bag around the axe so it looked like the perfect carry case for a deadly weapon. “Just try not to draw attention to yourself or use it on anyone.” He ushered me out with a hand on the small of my back as I protested that I didn’t just use it against people who weren’t attacking me.

I was still trying to reassure him as we entered the sucking sensation of the portal and found ourselves suddenly on the mossy floor at the edge of the ballroom. Two guards were waiting in highly polished uniforms with shiny helmets and holding sharp looking spears. An older elf was stood next to them with a long list of names.

Ironfist rattled ours off to him and then we waited while he found us on the list and ticked us off slowly and deliberately. I almost got the feeling he was enjoying the power of delaying us. Our weapons caused some consternation with the guards but we protested vehemently that it was a cultural symbol rather than just an axe. I thought Ironfist outdid himself with dwarven arrogance and the elf clearly thought it was above his paygrade to force us to hand them over. He did, however, call over another elf in a military uniform as another group of guests appeared from a different portal.

This elf bowed and introduced himself as Captain of the guards. With a lot more authority, he informed us that we could not have weapons before the King. After more arguing, Ironfist gave way and he and I were led past the ballroom up a small flight of stairs. The Captain gestured to a room with a heavy wooden door carved with more leaves and one of the guards pushed it open.

"You can leave your weapons here for the duration of the Ball."

"But…" I tried.

"Or you can return to your rooms." It wasn't up for discussion.

"These are very valuable, can you assure us of their safety?" Ironfist was more of a diplomat than I was.

The Captain barked out an order in Elvish and a guard took up position next to the door. Unable to think of any more objections, Ironfist shrugged at me and entered the room. It was dark and utilitarian. As my eyes adjusted to the gloom, I realised it was an armoury of sorts. Spears lined one wall and dull swords were shelved on another next to bright helmets. Ironfist carefully chose a place for his pickaxe in a corner where it would be less obtrusive. I took Bane from its custom-made bag and reluctantly placed it next to the pickaxe. It blended in with the other weapons here.

With a nod, the Captain started to escort us back to the portals and the entrance to the Equinox Ball.

"Er, sorry, er, where's the little girl's room?" The Captain looked at me blankly. "You know, the loos? Toilets?"

"Yes, that way," he pointed up the stairs.

"Great, I'll be back soon." I scurried up the stairs. I noticed Ironfist and the Captain weren't moving and waved them away, "Please, don't wait." They started to move and I breathed a sigh of relief. I wasn't sure how long it would take me to manoeuvre my way out of the underwear underneath my dress to go to the toilet. As I mounted the stairs, I realised there were a lot of doors and no signs. I tried to think; if I were an elf, what would I carve on the door for a privy? None of the leaves looked particularly latrine like so I decided to try them all. The first door opened onto a cleaning cupboard with a whiff of lemon and pine. The second door was locked. I was about to walk away when something tingled my senses. It was elven magic but there was also something else, something older. As I was trying to figure out why it seemed familiar, a group of important looking elves sauntered down the stairs. I tried to blend in, but a red dress in a wooden hallway didn't give me much chance of success.

An elf I recognised as the King frowned at me and said something in Elvish to an elf next to him. I tried to look at the floor and wondered if I should bow when a bright voice asked what I was doing here. I looked up and, trying not to meet anyone's gaze, was forced to admit I was looking for the toilets. Someone gave me directions to the third door on the left and I hurried off, squeezing myself against the wall. I heard muttering behind me and when I looked back, the King was still frowning at me over his shoulder.

Magic was definitely at work. The bathroom looked too big to fit into the tree, with luxurious individual stalls outfitted with a toilet, sink and full length mirror with flattering lighting, all fashioned from wood. A thoughtful basket was placed discreetly on a shelf with deodorant, hand cream and a few other bits in it. After struggling with my dress and underwear, I finally managed to relieve my bladder and get myself back to the ball. It was a lot easier finding my way back to the ballroom, I just had to follow the stairs. I paused briefly by the locked door on my way down, but still couldn't place the magical sensation. I smiled and carried on as an attendant rushed past with a covered basket.

Against my wishes, the group had waited for me before entering the ballroom. Master Ironfist was looking a little strained.

"We thought you'd fallen in!" Aloora smiled.

"I said not to wait!" I hissed as Master Ironfist again had his hand on the small of my back, guiding me into the room. I had never been escorted anywhere before and cursed myself for not establishing some ground rules. Would he expect me to dance with him?

A herald interrupted my thoughts by announcing our names loudly to the already crowded room. Everyone turned to look as we entered. Whispers started immediately as they realised there was a dwarf present. I felt hot gazes of curiosity and some more hostile looks as we walked across the floor, which was now strewn with matted rushes. We were led across the room to a dais where a number of carved wooden thrones sat.

Another herald announced us again, "His Majesty King Lireath, his royal highness Prince Morthimas and the members of the Elven High Council, this is Master Ironfist, delegate of the dwarfs; Amethyst Haernson; Aloora Dragonquest and Dorothy March of the Magical Liaison Office."

Ironfist bowed low with a hand over his heart in the traditional dwarven fashion. No one had gone over protocol for meeting royal families with me so I copied him while Aloora and Dot sank into graceful curtsies.

"I trust everything is to your satisfaction?" the Prince asked with a smile. I let Ironfist answer for us.

"Did you find everything you needed?" the King had a glint in his eye and was looking straight at me.

I felt my cheeks heat. What was I meant to say to that? "Yes, er, thank you for the directions, er, your majesty." I sounded like a moron. Aloora saved me by saying something in Elvish that made everyone smile. Then we were whisked out of the reception line and left alone.

"What was that?"

My friend shrugged, "I said your sense of direction was better underground and then complimented the decorations."

I nodded, it was true but it didn't help the reputation I suspected I was quickly gaining for being an idiot. At least I wouldn't have to see any of the elven royal family again.

"Shall we?" Ironfist asked courteously, extending an arm to me.

I squared my shoulders like I was going into battle, "Let's do this."

Chapter 20

Away from the intimidating thrones and royal family, I allowed myself the time to stare around the room. A quartet was playing beautiful melodies in one corner on elven harps. The guests were mainly elves, dressed in beautiful flowing robes of every colour of the rainbow, trimmed with gold or silver brocade. There was some seriously expensive jewellery here too catching the subtle lighting warmly; most of the guests were wearing intricate circlets or tiaras that looked ancient. Knowing how long elves lived, they probably were centuries old. I smirked as I imagined elves receiving jewellery for their sweet sixteen or whatever the equivalent coming of age thing was for them. I mentioned my thoughts to Aloora and she nodded and began describing the coming of age ceremony for me.

On my other side, Master Ironfist was trying to point out various representatives to me. I nodded politely as I pretended to listen. I wasn't planning to talk to anyone I didn't have to. Then I spotted the food. Long tables were set up along one side of the room, laden with full plates. I interrupted Ironfist, "Perhaps it would be easier to mingle near the buffet?"

He nodded enthusiastically, "Great idea Amethyst, we'll make a diplomat of you yet." He seemed to be being sincere and led the way to the table, smiling and nodding at everyone we passed. We manoeuvred around the dancefloor where couples were dancing gracefully in time to the music. Aloora fell into step behind me, her eyes bright as she gazed around the room. She was in her element. Dot followed, her eyes scanning the crowd.

I asked her what she was searching for and she shrugged, "Just habit."

Once at the table, my own enthusiasm subsided. It was all delicate creations in tiny portions. I risked a pink one and screwed my face up at the sharp taste of some sort of fish mixed with seaweed. Ironfist was loading himself a gold place with relish and giving me a running commentary on how amazing it was to be treated to elven delicacies. I watched with amusement as he tried the pink stuff and his face changed. Dwarf-fully, he finished it and looked round for a drink.

I gestured to one of the servers hovering around the edges with silver platters of champagne and mead. He ignored me so I marched up to him and pointedly retrieved two glasses of fizz with a smile before returning to Ironfist. The dwarf thanked me and downed his glass.

"I have never before tried pescaliqua, it was…quite the experience."

"You don't have to be diplomatic with me; it was awful!"

“Ms Haernson!” I shrugged and turned back to the buffet trying to find something more appetising. I found something that looked a little like the pasties I’d tried earlier. I nibbled it cautiously and was rewarded with the creamy cheese taste I had hoped for.

“Try these, they’re just cheese and something.”

Ironfist looked at me dubiously and took a bite. Satisfied it was nowhere near as bad as the fishy one, he abandoned his previous plate and surreptitiously took a new one. I wandered along the table until I found the desserts. I was more confident I’d like the sweets so I helped myself. I offered one to Dot but she declined.

“I ate earlier.”

I shrugged, “Your loss.”

She laughed at that then her eyes widened, “Is that Cirian?”

I turned to where she was looking. If it wasn’t the elven popstar, it looked a lot like him. “Why don’t you go and say hi?”

Dot made a spluttering sound. I regarded her. I hadn’t realised she was such a fan. A familiar voice called my attention, “Two dwarves, a gnome and a vampire? A most unusual start to a joke...” I turned with a smile to greet the elf. He was wearing a floor-length tweed robe. You could take the elf out of academia but you couldn’t take the academic out of the elf. Thankfully his robe didn’t have leather patches on the elbows.

“Professor Maron!”

"The one and only. You remember Mei?" he patted the hand of a small lady in a black fitted dress with a large Chinese dragon embroidered over it. I nodded and said hello to the curator.

"What are you doing here?"

"Well, Elrond owed me after the debacle with my exhibit…" she started with a smile at the elderly Professor. I had forgotten his first name was Elrond, a common elven name apparently.

"Oh I haven't missed an Equinox Ball for the past two hundred years! But what are you doing here, that is the question?" The elderly elf stroked his long white moustache.

"We helped the elves find a lost dragon egg so this is our reward."

His keen ears picked up on my disdain, "You do not care for celebrations?"

"Not ones where I'm clearly not welcome," I swept my gaze deliberately round the room. People were either staring openly at us or pointedly ignoring our small party.

"I think you'll find that it is nothing more than curiosity of the unknown, there are several academic works on the subject…"

Aloora saved me from a lecture by appearing at his elbow, "Professor! It's so great to see you. I have so much to tell you. I have more live recordings of the dragons to share and I think I managed to decipher some words this time…wait, is that the Dean of Oxford University?!"

The Professor laughed, “Let me introduce you.” They walked into the throng together, three heads bowed close as they discussed the latest advances in their shared Draconic research.

I shook my head and watched them go. I turned to get another drink and nearly choked on the sip when a deep voice spoke near my ear, “You’re doing great.”

I turned and looked at the slim face of Prince Morthimas. I made a high pitched spluttering sound. Should I bow? “Your highness,” I managed.

He covered my blustering by carrying on talking, “Morty. Call me Morty. They’re all enraptured by you, fascinated even.” I didn’t know how to respond to that but Morthimas carried on, “Do you know I hate these things? There’s so much expectation but nothing ever happens…until this year. First ball I’ve been to with dwarves. Some excitement at last. Maybe the older ones are getting over their prejudices. Long may it continue.” He raised his glass to mine in a toast. He seemed to want to talk, “That’s the trouble with this place, it’s so remote and everyone’s seen everything before. It’s…dull.”

“Don’t you like being a prince?”

“Not really. Everyone’s always looking at me like I should be doing something wise or regal. Or they want to get close to me to ask a favour. It’s all so…political,” he spat the word. “It’s why I’m glad my cousin has you.”

“What?”

“He said he feels like he can be himself with you. That’s rare. He’s a lucky elf.” Morthimas drained his glass while I reeled from that revelation. I'd thought he hadn't said anything about me. "Well, do you want to dance?"

"Wha?"

"Come on, it would really give them something to talk about if a dwarf danced with the elven prince."

"Er…" I opened my mouth to say I didn't dance.

"She would be honoured," Ironfist elbowed me in the ribs and thrust me forward. I glared at him over my shoulder as the prince led me to the wooden dancefloor set up near the quartet. They were playing a cheerful waltz and Morthimas took the lead, manoevering me across the floor with graceful ease. I caught more whispers and mutterings as elves passed by in a blur. The music came to an end and then we were standing apart clapping. I began to head away from the dancefloor and the attention.

Lorandir appeared in front of me with a smile, standing in front of his cousin who smiled behind his back and walked away. Lorandir took my hand and bowed slightly, "May I have this dance?"

They quartet had struck up a slow tune and other couples were swaying in time to the music.

"I, er, don't know the steps," I tried lamely. Why did this feel more intense than dancing with the prince?

"Just hold my hand like this," he pressed my palm to his, "and your other hand here." He placed my hand on his shoulder and then moved his own to my waist. He led me in what I guessed was a waltz. It was easy to get lost in his green eyes so I stopped looking at them and instead focused on a spot just above his shoulder. The music ended with a flourish and after a second's pause, he released my waist. He bowed over my hand again and this time pressed his lips against my palm. It was romantic and intimate. Heat coursed through me as I felt a blush creep up my body. I noticed others looking at us with wide eyes.

"I need a drink," I headed for one of the servers and claimed a glass of something cold. I downed it and took another. My dwarven blood was already making me overheat in the crowded ballroom and the dance had just turned up the heat a notch. Lorandir was beside me before I could drink my second glass. He started to say something but was dragged away by a uniformed elf murmuring something in his ear. He whispered his apologies to me and walked away. I watched him go and finished my drink. I needed to slow down or I'd disgrace myself, not to mention all of dwarfkind, by falling over again. My thoughts were interrupted by an elf in a bright green floor-length robe with jewelled emerald slippers on his feet. I stared at them as he came to a stop beside me, trying to mentally calculate the value of the stones.

"Is it true you made that necklace?"

I jerked my head up and followed his gaze to where Aloora was sparkling among a crowd of elves in their flowing robes and humans in black tie attire. It looked like she was engaging in some scholarly debate as she punctuated her points with her small hands. I nodded warily.

"It's amazing! And is it really a dragon scale?!"

I made an affirmative noise.

“Belzar, it’s real!” The elf shouted. Several of his friends instantly joined us and began crowding me with questions.

“How did you find a dragon scale?”

“What did you use to set it?”

“Can you make me one?”

This was too much. “Er, excuse me, I just, er, need some air.” I fled through the nearest opening in the root walls and found myself outside. I walked over to a thoughtful balcony created by more smooth roots and leaned on it, enjoying the crisp night air. My gaze travelled upwards past the treetops to the darkening night sky. Undimmed by competition with electric lights, the stars seemed brighter than I’d ever seen them.

I took a breath, savouring the peacefulness. If I didn’t have to attend that dzraking ball, this would be a lovely night. A cough sounded behind me. I turned quickly, my hand reaching for where Bane should have been. I sighed in relief as I recognised Lorandir. Curse his light elven footsteps.

“I thought you might like another drink.”

I took the glass and gratefully sipped from it. It was spring water, cool and refreshing. I put the glass to one side on the balcony and turned to admire the view.

“It’s beautiful, isn’t it?”

“I wish I knew the names of the constellations, it seems wrong to look at them without knowing what they are.”

“In Elvish, they are given names from our oldest tales. Some believe that heroes’ souls live in the stars.”

“Really?” I was intrigued.

Lorandir stepped up behind me and lowered his mouth to my ear, "That bright one there is the star of Novareth, follow it down and you can see his legendary bow and there is his mount, the sliver stag. See the stars forming the antlers?"

I followed his hand, trying to make out the pictures he was describing. "What about that one?"

He tucked a tendril of hair that had come loose behind my ear, "In English, that is the planet Mars, but we have another name for it. It is named for our goddess of love, Meerena, because it is both fiery and beautiful, like all women worth courting. Her story is not without sadness though. It is said that she loved an elf once and favoured him above all others. This caused great jealousy among gods and elves alike and one god took it upon himself to separate them. He tricked her into joining him in the heavens and then refused to allow her to leave. So she pined for her lover and caused a celestial war between gods and goddesses who did not like to be controlled. It lasted an age and her lover died before it was finished. As a reward for his faithfulness, she granted him life eternal as a star and now he lives beside her every night, favoured by her glory."

He had rested his hands either side of me on the balcony and I turned in the circle of his arms. Without thinking I tilted my head up to his. Music from the ballroom swirled softly around the night air. Then we were kissing. I parted my lips and deepened the kiss, pressing against him and pulling him towards me under the stars. He moaned softly and picked me up so I was sitting on the balcony. His moans deepened into a roar. I broke away, confused. The angry roar continued. We both looked up at the starlit sky.

The silhouette of a dragon flew low overhead.

Chapter 21

With a shriek of rage, the creature disappeared behind the Evergreen palace. Red leaves cascaded down as it turned tightly and circled back. It swooped low and crashed through the newly formed root walls.

The sound of wood splintering drew Lorandir and me from our shock. I raced inside. I tripped over my low heels. With a curse, I removed them and carried on running. The dragon was so huge that only half of it fit in the ballroom. Light reflected from its pale scales. A strange disco-ball effect at odds with the chaos. Well-dressed guests were screaming and fleeing or pressing themselves against the walls, trying to blend in with the décor.

I scanned the room. "Come on, come on…." There! I spotted Aloora and Dot ushering people out. I moved quickly and quietly over to them.

The dragon roared. My ears rang. It loosed off a bolt of ice in the room. Elves jumped aside agilely. It shrieked again and reared its head. It spewed a jet of acid green poison across the room. People screamed as the splashback burned through their fancy clothes. It was the female.

"What does it want?"

"Its egg…it thinks its egg is here," I hadn't really expected a reply and looked at Aloora strangely. She was dazed and shaking her head. "I can understand it Ame," I didn't like the way her eyes were shining.

"Not the time Ally!" Something pinged in my head. The unusual magic I had been trying to place earlier reminded me of the dragon. "Try not to let anyone get killed!" I hoisted up my ball-gown and ran out of the room to the stairs. I sprinted up them. I paused by the armoury. No one was guarding it now. I pushed the door. It was locked. I breathed out a Dwarfish curse then rummaged in my small, impractical bag. It was barely big enough to hold anything useful, but I had stashed my phone and keys in there out of habit. I grabbed my keys and held up the enchanted one I used for the locks on my own shop. It was time to find out if it worked on elven doors. After a couple of seconds concentrating, I heard a satisfying click. I tried the door and it opened soundlessly. I retrieved my axe and immediately felt better with its weight in my hands. Armed, I stepped back outside. I followed the tingle of elven magic to the door I had tried earlier.

The room was still locked. I pressed my key into a knot of wood that looked like it might be a keyhole and tried to drown out the screams from downstairs. The door gave a creak. I pushed it hard. I misjudged the weight of the wooden door and stumbled into a storeroom.

An unusual feel of magic tickled my senses. I closed my eyes. Elven illusion magic mixed with something else, something older and more reptilian. It seemed to be coming from a box stored low on the shelves. I opened my eyes and reached for it. I peeled back the lid. A glow seemed to emanate from it. The dragon egg! I closed the lid and picked up the box. I wedged it under my arm, grabbed a handful of skirt. With Bane in my other hand, I stepped back out onto the stairs.

The Captain of the guards was standing outside, giving orders to his elves. Schiztz. I pressed myself to the wall and edged behind him back to the ballroom.

"Stop! What are you doing?"

I turned and tried to look innocent, "Oh, just going back to the ball…" I stepped backwards slowly. One step. Another step.

"I said stop! Why have you got your axe?"

I looked down at my hand, "Er, there's a dragon…"

He seemed torn between his orders that guests shouldn't be armed and the inescapable fact that there was no longer any ball. "What's in that box?"

"Er…" I gave up and legged it down the stairs. It was foolish to try to outrun an elf. He was on me before I got three steps.

"Please, it's what it wants!" I tried to keep hold of it but he prised it from my grasp. Two guards pinned my arms to my sides.

He opened it slowly, mistrusting me. His eyes widened when he saw the bejewelled egg inside. "How…?"

"I don't know, but the dragon is here for the egg. Please! We can give it back…"

The Captain looked at the door I had left open, "The King… he told me to lock that room and make sure no one went inside…"

"I don't know anything about that!"

"He ordered me…"

"Please! You have a choice, we can save those people."

His eyes glinted with the glow of the egg. I struggled against the guards holding my arms. They were stronger than me and I had no chance. I saw his fists clench on the box. He nodded and I was free.

"We will escort you," with that, the box was back in my hands. I shifted the grip on my axe and headed back downstairs with the elves in tow. They shouldered a path for me through the fleeing ball goers and we were back in the ballroom. Torn fabric littered the frosty floor. Aloora, Dot and Gunther were crouched under a table with Lorandir. I smiled and stepped forward.

"Stop! What are you doing?!" A shout from behind the throne made me pause. The King stepped out from his hiding place. "That is mine!"

"It belongs to the dragon!" I shouted back clearly. The dragon stopped moving. It watched me with its emerald eyes. Icy vapour steamed from its nostrils. I stepped over broken glass and wooden shards into the middle of the ballroom. It flared its nostrils at me and gave a low, guttural growl. I placed the box reverently down and stepped back. It narrowed its eyes and continued growling.

Aloora was somehow by my side. She said something in Draconic, her words twisting into strange sounds. The dragon snorted and reached a long talon to her neck. Aloora said something else and it seemed to regard her intelligently. It reached towards me and then down, delicately destroying the box around the egg. It breathed out a cloud of icy spray and all elven magic around the egg disappeared. The full force of draconic magic swept over me. It was majestic.

The female dragon crooned at the egg in a strange high-pitched song. I stood in awe. It reached for the egg with its front feet. I stepped back warily. That's when I noticed the King edging forward. A crazed look lit up his face. Somehow he was holding a curved elven sword.

"It's mine! I will be the first dragon rider in millennia and all glory shall be mine!"

"Dad?" Prince Morthimas called from the dais.

I stared at the King, snaking towards the egg. Surely this idiot hadn't really thought he could kidnap a dragon's egg and raise a live dragon unnoticed, let alone ride the dzraking thing.

The King let off a blast of magic, creating a shield between the egg and the dragon. The female roared and bared its sharp teeth. She forced her way further into the ballroom. The tree shook dangerously. Wood splintered from the ceiling with a painful creak. I heard a cry from Aloora as she was knocked aside by a chunk of falling debris. She lay still. I took one step towards her. With a burst of ice, the dragon blasted through the elf's shield. Morthimas was by his father's side, trying to pull him away. Dot was with Aloora, tugging her to safety. I turned back to the dragon, edging backwards. I saw the dragon take a deep breath. It aimed directly at Lorandir's cousin.

"No!" I shouted and spoke the Dwarfish word to activate Bane's shield. I dived in front of the Prince. My side burst with pain as I landed hard on a large splinter of wood. Unfortunately, this meant I was now also in front of the King; the object of the dragon's rage.

I turned my back to the dragon, "Get out of here!" I waved frantically at Morthimas. He was torn between leaving his father and surviving a dragon attack. I felt the shield weaken as an icy blast hit it. I dragged the Prince to his feet and pushed him away. Dot was there in an instance and sped him to relative safety. While I was watching the Prince, the King swung for my jaw. I ducked instinctively and was met with a knee to my face. My vision sparked red. "You moron, it's going to kill you!" I tried to say. It came out as garbled sounds with my jaw ringing from the impact.

The dragon's magic was pressing against the shield. I could feel my magic weakening.

"Get out of there!" I heard someone cry.

I felt the shield give way. I staggered to the side. Too late. There was a hiss of poison. I screamed in pain as it burnt through my dress and skin. Freezing cold surrounded me as the dragon exhaled a blast of ice at point blank range. I felt my amethyst pendent heat comfortingly around my neck. It distracted me a little from the dagger-like pain scraping across my skin. Then it went black.

Chapter 22

I woke up slowly, keeping my eyes closed and enjoying the feel of expensive linen sheets against my naked skin. Naked? How much had I had to drink last night that I was sleeping in the nude? I moved my hands experimentally over my body. Ah. Not naked. The silky nightdress had worked its way up, exposing my entire lower half. Satisfied with that, I blinked my eyes open.

Wasn't the window on the other side of the room yesterday? I didn't know much about elven architecture, but did rooms really rearrange themselves overnight? I blinked some more as my eyes adjusted to the morning glow coming from the window. The duvet had an unfamiliar pattern of oak leaves and acorns swirling over it. My brain caught up with my eyes. I was in someone else's room. Schiztz.

I slowly turned my head to the other side of the large bed. Sure enough, a head was lying on the pillow. Lorandir. Schiztz, schiztz, schiztz. How much had I had to drink at the banquet? Curious, I lifted the covers slightly and peeked underneath. He was naked from the waist up, and his muscles were well defined even when asleep. From the waist down, he was wearing plain, drawstring pyjama trousers. Maybe we didn't sleep together then.

I slowly wriggled my way to the edge of the bed.

"Good morning," his voice startled me and I jumped. As I was right at the edge, this also meant I fell off onto the wooden floor. "Are you ok?"

I blushed bright red, adjusted my nightdress and rushed to the door. I fervently hoped this room was a mirror of mine and there was a bathroom in there. I pulled it open and dived inside. It was a bathroom. The only difference between this and the one in my room was the scent. A masculine mix of leather and the smell of a forest after a summer downpour: fresh and leafy. It was delicious. I gazed longingly at the carved, wooden bathtub but I guessed it would be odd to take a long soak in someone else's bathroom.

After using the facilities, I sank against the table holding the sink to give myself a moment to think. I met my gaze in the mirror and moaned. My carefully applied make-up had slipped during the night and my eyes were surrounding by a ring of mascara. My lipstick was smudged around my mouth. My hair had partially come out of the complicated plaits that the elves had created and was a mess of tangles and half braids. I unplaited the remaining braids and searched for a hairbrush, feeling like I was prying as I opened cupboards quietly.

I found a wooden handled brush tucked neatly inside a cabinet, next to full bottles of that same scented shower gel. It had an intricate celtic knot pattern detailed on the handle and strong bristles. I winced as I forced the wooden brush through my hair and it caught on the tangles. After I'd finished, I washed my face carefully, getting rid of my untidy make up. The pristine white flannel I'd used was now stained. I threw it in the laundry basket.

As I was about to unlock the door, I noticed an emerald green fluffy dressing gown hanging on a hook. I put it on. It complimented the green silk nightdress perfectly. I tied the belt into a tight knot, took a deep breath, squared my shoulders and went back into the bedroom.

Lorandir was sitting upright in bed. He quirked an eyebrow at me but his voice was tense, "I thought you'd fallen in."

I smiled before I could help it. I perched on the edge of the bed and refused to meet his eyes, "Last night…"

He just smiled at me. I noticed the dark smudges under his eyes. "How do you feel?"

"Did we…er…what happened?" I was annoying myself now.

"What do you remember?"

I twisted the covers between my fingers and bit my lip as I thought, "Er, well there was the ball, and we, er, kissed…and…wait, was there a dragon?" A huge white dragon with shining scales burst into my memory.

He took pity on me, seeing I was genuinely discombobulated, "There was a dragon. You returned its egg."

"The King?! Did he really want to be a dragon rider?!" I interrupted, another memory surfacing.

Lorandir shook his head, “He was a power hungry fool. He’d ordered the original Captain of the guards to steal the egg, the Captain confirmed it to the Office. We were keeping an eye on Lireath anyway but no one was able to prove anything.”

“Was?”

“He’s gone. You’re lucky you’re still alive. You shouldn’t go being a hero for people who don’t deserve it.”

Memories began to bubble in my mind, “What…but Morthimas was innocent…”

He moved closer to me, “Morty was long gone. You took a shot of poison for the King and then were frozen by the dragon. You only survived because you were wearing your amethyst,” my hand instinctively went to my neck where my amethyst pendant was still hanging on its delicate chain, “I don’t know how that works but…we managed to free you, but…I thought you were gone.” He choked back a sob.

“Hey, I’m still here,” I reached for his hand and gave it an encouraging squeeze, “it’ll take more than a pissed off dragon to get rid of me.”

He squeezed my hand back at the bad joke, and wiped his face with the back of his hand, “Our best healers poured magic into you, but a dragon’s poison is potent. I’ve been keeping the magic topped up all night. How do you feel?”

“Good,” I rolled my shoulders.

“Can I check your back? That’s where the poison hit you?”

I nodded and he moved closer to sit behind me. Delicately, gently, he pulled the dressing gown from my shoulders. I felt heat spreading through my body. He traced his fingers over my back. I felt his magic flow through me with its familiar sensation of bittersweet dark chocolate, honey mead and sunlit forests. I closed my eyes and leaned backwards as he felt for any lingering traces of poison.

I moaned slightly and he moved behind me, starting to rub my shoulders and leaning his mouth close to my neck. "I was so worried," he murmured, planting a kiss on my neck. Pleasant warmth flowed through me as he kissed me again.

Aloora burst through the door at that intimate moment and he shifted himself so he could examine my back. I felt a blush heating my face as she stared at me. Lorandir lifted the sleeves of the dressing gown up so I was fully covered and stood. He nodded at Aloora as he strode to the bathroom.

"Well, I had come to check if you were ok, but by the looks of it, you're much better!"

I put my head in my hands. She enveloped me in a hug, "Thank goodness you're alright."

A memory surfaced, my friend being knocked to the floor, I pulled back and met her gaze, "Are you ok?"

She waved me off dismissively, "I'm fine. I'm not the heroine who decided to throw herself in front of that dzraking king!"

"I'm not a heroine…"

"No, you're an idiot! I thought I'd lost you, don't ever do that to me again!" she hugged me again, then pulled back and wiggled her eyebrows, "Now, catch me up on you and Lorandir..."

I coloured again and shook my head, “Nothing happened.”

She gave me a playful punch on the arm, “You’re seriously telling me that you shared a bedroom with that gorgeous creature and nothing happened?”

I shook my head again, “I was passed out you know…” I bit my lip, “…unfortunately!”

She laughed, “Well I’d better go then, so you can get on with seducing the scrumptious elf!”

I shushed her, “He can probably hear you, you know?!”

Aloora laughed again, then her voice turned serious, “You’re really ok?”

I nodded, “I’m ok, confused about…” I gestured to the bathroom door, “but ok.”

She raised her eyebrows playfully, “Well, what usually happens when a girl likes a boy is…”

I launched a pillow at her. She caught it and threw it back at me. She threw surprisingly hard for such a petite gnome. “Seriously Ame, what are you confused about? He likes you, you like him. Simples.” For someone who loved complicated academic papers, she was really able to get to the point. I screwed up my face, was it that simple? She shook her head at me, “For someone who says she wants a simple life, you are seriously overcomplicating this!”

That was so similar to what I had been thinking about her that I smiled again, it was good to have a best friend who knew me so well.

“If you’re really better, I’m going to leave you to it and get to the library.”

"I'm really better," I reassured her.

She left, calling out "Don't overcomplicate it!" as she closed the door noisily.

I groaned and fell back on the bed. I just wanted to crawl under the covers. Lorandir opened the bathroom door sheepishly, confirming my suspicions that he could hear the entire conversation.

"Soooo…" I started eloquently.

"Soooo…" he echoed, coming to lie next to me on the bed. I stared at the high wooden ceiling, tracing the knots in the wooden arches with my eyes. He propped himself up onto his elbow and reached over to turn my face so I met his green eyes.

"Amethyst," he started, his low voice making my name sound sexy, "I care about you and I'd like to see where this goes," I didn't reply, I was too busy watching his kissable lips. He took my silence for refusal, "but I understand if the differences between us are too much for you."

My heart clenched in my chest. Yes we were from two different worlds in one way, but we weren't really so different and at the thought of losing him, I realised I really liked him, even if he was an arrogant elf at times. I leaned into him and kissed him hard. I was taking a chance on us.

Epilogue

It was finally moving day. I had helped load Marco's small Volkswagen with boxes of books and clothes and volunteered to take the bus so he could fit more in. I settled into the uncomfortable fabric seat and watched the city scenery roll by as adjacent conversations rolled over me.

"Your top's too short for that outfit!"

"No it isn't, I've got leggings on!"

"If your leggings are transparent, they're not leggings, they're tights!"

I turned surreptitiously to look at the two women. They looked in their twenties and I could confirm with one glance that one of them was indeed wearing a pair of transparent leggings with a tight fitted vest top and cropped jacket. I had an unflattering view of her thong. I looked away quickly before they noticed me staring.

The bus stopped in the bay and I heaved my carryall over my shoulder. I didn't have much in the way of physical possessions now, especially after another one of my tops had been destroyed by a chimera, but my trusty axe was in there. I was never going out without it again!

I walked through the drizzle over Cardiff Bay to the apartment building. Mr Davies, the Arcade's owner, had told me it would be at least six months before the shop was habitable again and he didn't want to risk getting into trouble with the authorities. My previous illicit flat wasn't an option. It had been an easy choice to accept Aloora and Marco's offer of a room with them especially as Aloora had signed the contract before the estate agent had realised that the dragons had gone and he could put the price up. And the rent split three ways was even more palatable for us all, even with the extra deposit I had to put in so we could have Errol with us. I was looking forward to picking up my small wyrm next weekend, once we had unpacked a bit.

Plus, Lorandir had a flat in the Bay and I had a feeling I was going to be spending a lot of time there, if the past month had been anything to go by.

Things weren't just looking up in the romance department either. Ever since Aloora had shown off the collar I had made her at the Equinox Ball, I had several expensive commissions, all arranged through social media. Gunther was still allowing me to use some workspace at his warehouse, although I'd forced him to accept some rent for that as soon as the insurance payment came through. It wasn't the same as my own shop, but it was working for now.

I waded through the piles of boxes and dumped my bag in my room. It was the smallest one, without a great view but it still fitted a double bed comfortably. I bumped into Aloora on the way out.

"Hey roomy!"

"Hey you! I was wondering when that bus would turn up. Fancy helping me organise my book collection?"

"Er…"

"I've told Marco we need a shopping trip to get more furniture; I even offered to drive but for some reason he said we'd do it later in the week!"

"Er…" I may have told Marco about some of the trips I'd had where my best friend was driving. I may have used words like 'terrifying'. I wasn't surprised he didn't want to hand over the keys to his car.

I headed back down to find Marco and help unload.

"Pizza tonight!" Aloora called after me.

I had a feeling things were going to work out.

***

In the dark room of the club, the elf winced from the verbal tongue lashing he'd been given. There were others gathered around the large table, but the elf focused only on one.

"Director, please, another chance is all I need."

It was the wrong choice of words. The Director didn't like weakness of any kind. His eyes narrowed as he stared at the elf. The Director purposefully adjusted the neat Windsor knot in his silk tie before he spoke. The gesture brought images of the long fingers winding around the elf's neck and, unthinking, the elf lifted his delicate hand to his own throat and swallowed nervously.

"You have failed in your task and we can only hope Lireath did not confide in anyone else about your council. If there are any suspicions about us or our purpose it would jeopardise our goal…but you are fortunate. It would draw too much attention for you to go missing when a new king is about to be elected. You will stay on the Elven High Council…for now."

"Yes, yes, of course. I await your command."

"You are dismissed."

The elf almost sank to the ground in relief. He forced his legs to stay straight and then turned at the sucking sound of a portal opening behind him. It shimmered like liquid oil above a silver metal box. He stepped through quickly before the Director changed his mind. Only once he was back in his own home and sure he was alone, did the elf allow himself to collapse.

Thank you for reading book two in the Rise of Dragons series. If you enjoyed this book, you can get a free prequel to my Rise of Dragons series at my website (www.gemmaclatworhty.com) and join the conversation at Gemma's book wyrms .

As an independent author, your reviews help me decide which series to keep going so please do leave one for Equinox Betrayal and if you enjoyed this book, try Darkest Deception, book four in the Rise of Dragons series.

Books in the Rise of Dragons series:

Awakening

Solstice of Dragons

Equinox Betrayal

Darkest Deception

About the Author

Gemma started writing during the 2020 lockdown and loves fantasy fiction and dragons in particular. She lives in Wiltshire with her family and two cats and also enjoys crafts of all kinds. Join the conversation at Gemma's book wyrms readers' group on Facebook.

She also writes children's books. You can find out more on her website www.gemmaclatworthy.com or follow her on patreon (www.patreon.com/G_Clatworthy) Instagram (www.instagram.com/gemmaclatworthy) or Facebook (www.facebook.com/gemmaclatworthy).

www.ingramcontent.com/pod-product-compliance
Ingram Content Group UK Ltd.
Pitfield, Milton Keynes, MK11 3LW, UK
UKHW040005200726
13854UKWH00001B/49

9 781915 516039